Abigail's
REVENGE
PAT BALLARD

PEARLSONG
PRESS

Pearlsong Press
P.O. Box 58065
Nashville, TN 37205
www.pearlsong.com
1-866-4-A-PEARL

© 2005 Patricia F. Ballard
www.patballard.com

ISBN-13: 978-1-59719-003-9
ISBN-10: 1-59719-003-9
Library of Congress Control Number: 2005907297

Original trade paperback

Other books by Pat Ballard published by Pearlsong Press:

Dangerous Curves Ahead: Short Stories
Wanted: One Groom
Nobody's Perfect
His Brother's Child
A Worthy Heir

Prologue

Despair settled over Abigail Avery like the thick fog that was moving in and engulfing the valley outside the dingy kitchen window.

Her father had finally fallen into the drunken sleep that claimed him every night after supper. She listened to his ragged breathing, and knew that he'd be kicked back in that horrible old recliner that he refused to let her throw away. Just like he'd forbidden her mom to touch it when she was still alive.

Abigail raised a work-reddened hand and touched the soft, pulpy area around her right eye. It would be blue by morning, from the impact of his balled up fist, which had slammed against her face because she'd burned the cornbread.

Oh! How she hated that man! It would be so easy to kill him as he lay there in his drunken state. He'd never know what hit him.

She took the shotgun from the rack where it hung over the kitchen door. The cold metal of the barrel sent a thrill through her. She slid her hands up and down the smooth shaft as if she were caressing a lover. A smile almost made it to her full lips, almost brought a light to her dull, smoky blue eyes, when she thought of the freedom this object could bring her. Almost. But Abigail Avery didn't remember how to smile. Smiling was as foreign to her as knowing how to live without fear.

She raked her hand through her unkempt, golden-red hair as a shudder wrenched her skinny frame. *Maybe tomorrow,* she thought, as she pushed through the squeaky back door and headed for the barn to finish her chores.

Night was closing in. The fog added an eerie cast to the old barn, which was about a hundred yards from her house. It nestled picturesquely in the little valley of green pasture that separated the house and barn from the dense woods that surrounded them.

She should be afraid to be out here alone, this time of day. She sensed there were reasons for her to be afraid. But for Abigail, there was nothing out here that could possibly be any worse than what she'd just left behind. And, besides that, she had her friend with her. Her shotgun.

She stood the gun just inside the barn door and made her way to Betsy's stall. The cow watched her approach with huge, sad brown eyes. Abigail knew that Betsy would soon "dry up" and wouldn't be able to provide the milk they depended on from her.

Abigail's dad had sold Betsy's calf a few weeks ago, saying they couldn't afford to feed both animals. Actually, they couldn't afford to feed Betsy as much as she needed. A fact that the cow's emaciated frame made apparent.

She caressingly brushed her fingers across the skinny ribs of the hungry cow and felt guilty as she sat down on the stool to try and leach out enough milk for her father's breakfast.

"I'm sorry, old girl," she cooed, as her cold fingers wrapped around the wrinkled teats of the faithful animal. Betsy drew in a long breath and let it out slowly, as if she were trying to push as much milk out as she could for Abigail.

Abigail's hands froze in mid-squeeze. She could never mistake the familiar squeak of the barn door being slowly opened. There was barely enough light left in the old building for Abigail to see Betsy and the milk pail, so she couldn't see the door. What had caused it to squeak? Had someone come in, or had the wind just moved it?

Her gun! She'd left the gun standing just inside the door, like she did every day. Could she make it to the gun if someone was in the barn with her? She had to try.

Easing the milk pail down and quietly standing up from the stool, she silently made her way to the door. Enough dusty light sifted through the cracks of the aged building to let her see that no one was around. Heaving a sigh of relief, she hastened to the place where she'd left the shotgun. She could have found it if she'd been blind. She went through the same routine every night. Placed the weapon in the same spot night after night, as if just having it leaning against the wall would protect her. She reached the spot where she'd left it and grabbed thin air. The gun was gone.

Flattening her thin body against the weathered boards, she strained her eyes, willing them to see something—anything, any movement, any shadows from the interior of the barn.

Nothing.

Then she heard it. The unmistakable sound of a shotgun being fired.

The sound came from the house. Not taking time to think, Abigail broke into a run. As she reached the back door, some semblance of sanity caused her to stop. She couldn't just rush in and accost the person who had fired the gun! But *who* had fired the gun? And at *what?*

She eased to the kitchen window and peeked inside. Nothing seemed out of place. Making her way farther around the house, she stopped and peered through each window, still finding nothing out of the ordinary. Darkness, thickened by the fog, had settled around her. Shivering from the unknown, Abigail hesitantly made her way up the steps, across the front porch, and quietly pushed her way through the front door.

Her eyes fastened on the scene she had played over and over in her mind, but never actually expected to see. A blood-soaked hole in her father's recliner exactly where his head should have been.

Particles of hair, skin, and other matter that Abigail didn't want to put a name to dripped from and clung to the dirty, age-worn leather of the old chair. Her shotgun lay across the top of his lifeless hands. There was no way he had shot himself. Someone had killed him and placed her gun on his body.

Abigail became aware of distant sirens. But how? Their farm was too far away from anyone's house for the shot to have been heard. And even if someone had heard the shot and called it in, there wasn't enough time for the sheriff to already get out here from town.

Eighteen-year-old Abigail Avery, who knew almost nothing about life, knew, in that instant, that she was going to prison for murder. She just didn't know why.

It took the jury exactly twenty minutes to return a verdict of voluntary manslaughter. Judge Haney asked her to stand as he read her thirty-year prison sentence.

As he read, Abigail looked the jurors directly in the eyes and promised each one of them, silently, individually, that she would be back.

Bile, hot and burning, rose in Desh Elliot's throat as he watched the hairy hand of Sheriff William Lucas guide the beautiful mass of red hair into the patrol car. He knew it would be a long time before he would see that hair again. Hair that he'd watched blowing in the wind. Blazing in the sun. Falling gently around the beautiful face of the girl he'd loved ever since he could remember.

Love, unnoticed. Love, unreturned. Love, without hope. Because even as a child, and then as a young man, Desh Elliot knew that Abigail Avery didn't believe she was worthy of anyone's love. He knew, somehow, that she could not conceive of the idea that he, of all people, would love her.

Now, nineteen-year-old Desh Elliot knew what he must do with his life. While he waited for Abigail to serve her time in prison, while he waited for her to return to him, he knew what he must do.

For she would return. He was sure of that. He'd read and understood that message on her face as she'd stared down each juror. He had watched her enough, through the years, to read, feel, experience almost any emotion she could have.

And what she was promising those ass-kissing, paid-off jurors was that she would be back, and she would get to the bottom of this trumped-up charge against her.

Well, she wouldn't be alone when she returned. He'd make sure of that.

Chapter 1

Leaky Springs—30 miles. Abigail watched the sign go by as she shifted in the seat of the Greyhound bus bringing her back to the only place she'd ever known, except the prison she'd been in for the past ten years.

"Prison" is a harsh, scary word for some people, but for Abigail it had been a respite from the hell she'd grown up in. She soon found out that if she did what she was told, life was okay. At least when she did what she was told, she didn't get beat, anyway. There was always enough to eat, clothes to wear, and most of the time everyone left her alone.

And there was the library. The place that had become Abigail's best friend. She'd read every book in that library at least once, and some of them two times. Especially the law books. She'd studied and memorized cases where people had been railroaded into prison, like she had been. She'd embedded in her mind what her rights were as a wrongly imprisoned person. She knew how far she could go and how much she could get away with in the revenge department.

And now she was ready to wage war on a small Southern town. A backstabbing little hole-in-the-wall place that had no idea she was quickly making her way toward them to raise more hell than they'd seen in years.

She'd forced herself to stay on her best behavior in prison. Even when that bull-dyke Josey Jones put the make on her and she wanted nothing more than to slash her throat, Abigail managed to hold her temper and negotiate her way out of the situation. She found out that Josey had some nasty habits, like smuggling drugs into the prison, that she didn't want the warden to know about. So Abigail made a deal with her. She wouldn't tell anyone about the drugs if Josey kept her hands and mouth to herself. Josey knew that Abigail had wormed her way into the trust of the prison personnel, so she didn't have much of a choice. But on her last day, Abigail had told all. Let Josey suck on that!

So now, Abigail Avery was a free woman. Free. What a concept. A concept that she'd never experienced before. She'd never been free as a child. She'd been a slave to a mean, violent man who thought the women in his life were put on earth to wait on his sorry ass while he did nothing but make demands.

She'd read enough books to have an idea of what freedom meant, but when she tried to imagine it for herself, she felt no emotion. No sense of what it actually meant.

Probably because she still wasn't free. She was imprisoned by a determination to find out why she'd been sent to jail for a murder she didn't commit. She was consumed with the desire to get to the bottom of the mystery. To ferret out and make every jury member answer to her why they'd found her guilty, when they all knew she wasn't.

And she was coming back to Leaky Springs with an advantage. Hopefully, it would take the townspeople a while to recognize her.

To her amazement, when she'd started getting regular,

healthy meals, her body had filled out in all the right places. She'd changed from the emaciated slip of a girl who'd left town to a full-figured, well-endowed, voluptuous woman. At least, that's the way Josey had described her. The only thing that hadn't changed about Abigail was her hair, her mysterious blue eyes, and her flawless, fair complexion, which had gotten even better as her health improved.

The screeching of brakes brought Abigail out of her reverie. The bus pulled to a stop in the middle of the town square. Abigail's insides lurched to her throat as she became aware of the sameness of what she saw. After ten years, nothing seemed to have changed. Her heart pounded painfully as she stepped from the bus. This moment that she thought she'd been so ready for was scaring the hell out of her.

As she stepped from the bus, a gust of wind lifted her mane of red hair and swirled it around her head. Natural curls spiraled in all directions. She looked like Athena, the goddess of battle, with Medusa-like snakes twining around her head. And like Medusa, Abigail had returned to destroy—in order to recreate balance. To purify.

Desh Elliot's entire body jerked to attention when he glanced out of the window of his upstairs office in the century-old courthouse. Each morning as the Greyhound bus screeched to a stop, it was his habit to look down and see who got off the bus—wondering if each day would be the day she came home.

Today was the day. He'd recognize that hair anywhere! But the body was a body he would never have recognized. Full. Curvy. Luscious. His Abigail had grown up. And as recognition filled his brain, sexual awareness charged through his lower body. Abigail had *really* grown up!

And she was his, dammit! The thought of another man's hands on that body shot a blaze of anger through his system that staggered him. He had earned the right to claim her. He had loved her when no one else did. He had patterned his future life for her protection. Her liberation. Her exoneration.

As his eyes followed her progress across the street, he claimed her. Branded her as his. Desh Elliot had learned in the past ten years that he was a strong man. A man to be reckoned with. A man who got what he wanted. And he wanted Abigail Avery. He wanted her name cleared. He wanted the scheming, low-life crooks in this small town brought to their knees. And he wanted, finally, to hold Abigail Avery in his arms and tell her how much he'd always loved her.

He swiped a large hand through his blond hair, as a gleam formed in his emerald green eyes.

"It's time to get this show on the road," he growled in a sultry Southern drawl as he reached for the phone.

As Abigail stepped onto the sidewalk in front of what had always been Ma Tucker's Cafe, the sudden opening of the tat tered front door startled her. A burly man came out whom she immediately recognized as an older Judge Harry Haney, toothpick dangling from his fat, watery lips. Her steps almost faltered as she looked up into his sleazy brown eyes. Would he recognize her?

"Good morning!" he said, in a suggestive voice that Abigail remembered all too well.

"Hello," she mumbled, but didn't slow her pace.

"You're new in town, aren't you?"

She'd have to stop and answer him. If she didn't, it might throw suspicion on her. Thinking fast, she turned partially toward him and answered, "I'm just here for a few days checking out some real estate for a client."

He looked her up and down, and an old memory crept unwanted into her awareness. She fought to contain the shudder that threatened to vibrate her body. Fought to hide the contempt she felt for this slimy man.

"Oh? And where might this real estate be located?" His body tensed with total attention. Abigail was sure he didn't recognize her. He showed no awareness of who she was, but a great interest in what she was saying.

"Oh, nothing in particular," she covered quickly. "I just have a client that wants me to check to see if there's anything available in this area."

"Ain't nothing much for sale in these parts, so you might as well pass that on to your client. But if there's anything else I can help you with, just let me know," he said, giving her a knowing wink.

"Thanks," she answered, and left before he could say anything else. She felt his eyes on her until she rounded the corner of the building.

She would save him until last, she decided. She already had enough on him to bring him down, but she wanted to get more, if there was more. And she wanted him to sweat as he watched his cohort go down all around him. This was going to be so sweet.

As she headed out of town, she dreaded the long walk to the farm where she grew up. It was at least two miles, maybe more, she couldn't remember. But she didn't dare ask anyone to take her out there. That would make it too easy to guess who she was. She'd just have to walk.

She knew the house was still there. She knew because at least every six months since she'd been in prison she'd gotten a letter from Don Morrison, the only lawyer in Leaky Springs, requesting that she sell her property to the town. The letter always requested the "land and house," so she knew the house was still there. What she couldn't understand was why the small town of Leaky Springs was interested in buying her father's old rundown house and the forty acres of nothing that went with it.

That was almost as big a mystery to her as why she'd been framed and sent to prison. Was there a connection? The question had haunted her ever since she'd received the first attempt to buy the place, six months after she'd been imprisoned.

It was mid-April, but already getting humid and warm in southern Mississippi. Beads of sweat glistened on Abigail's forehead, and she quickly became aware of the rocks in the cheaply laid blacktop road as they ground into the thin soles of her shoes.

She set the suitcase with her few meager belongings in it on the ground, then carefully eased herself down on it to rest for a few moments. The distant chugging of a tractor brought back memories of a childhood when her mom was still alive and things weren't so bad for Abigail. Times when she was able to go outside and sit with her beat-up old rag doll and listen to the birds sing, and the neighbor plowing his field, getting ready to put the new crops in the ground.

So lost was she in her thoughts that the big black car was slowing to a stop beside her before she even noticed it.

"Would you like a ride, Miss?"

He was an old man now, Abigail realized, as she recognized Ted Elliot. His hair was snow white, and his eyes had taken on that bleary, watery look that some old people's eyes have. He'd been the principal of Leaky Springs High School. Might still be, for all she knew.

"Yes, I would love a ride, if you don't mind." Why not? She'd let him take her to the driveway of her old home. The house couldn't be seen from the driveway, so maybe he wouldn't connect the two of them. She doubted if he'd even known she existed as a person, much less where she had lived. The school hadn't taken a lot of interest in her, one way or another.

After placing her suitcase in the back seat of the car, she got in beside it and closed the door.

He didn't say a word. Didn't look at her. It was almost as

if he didn't remember she was in the car as he slowly navigated the narrow, curvy road, in some cases barely keeping the big car out of the deep ditches on each side.

As soon as she recognized the driveway to her house, she told him, "I'll just get out up here at this old rusty mailbox."

"Ah, yes. The mysterious Avery place," he mumbled, barely above a whisper.

"Mysterious?" she asked, as she opened the door to get out.

"Oh, don't mind me, missy, I'm just an old man who hears things when I shouldn't," he answered, and waited for her to get her suitcase. Obviously, for him, the conversation was over.

As Abigail watched the car disappear around a bend in the road, she had the sudden urge to run after him and make him talk to her. Did he really know something? Or was he just being dramatic?

Reluctantly, she turned and headed down the driveway. She'd walked several yards before she finally figured out what was niggling at her brain. She'd been gone from here for ten years. The property was still hers. So why was this driveway so well used? Multiple sets of tire marks made grooves in the sandy soil. Different types of tire marks. Who was using her driveway, and why?

With even more questions swirling around her head, Abigail stopped abruptly at the sight of the old house. It was the typical crackerbox style that was so popular in the rural South. Peeling paint had almost disappeared, leaving the weathered boards open and vulnerable to the elements. Oddly enough, all the windowpanes were still in place, with none broken. The steps that led up to the front porch were beginning to rot and crumble, but the boards on the porch still felt sturdy as she walked across to the front door.

Remembering what she had seen the last time she'd come

through this door, she was hesitant to push it open. Unlocked, it squeaked open at her touch, and she entered the dimly lit room. As her eyes adjusted to the faint light that filtered through the dirty windows, she could see that nothing had changed since the last time she was here, except ten years of dust that covering everything.

An old picture of her parents in their younger days still hung on the wall over the fireplace, just like it always had. That's one of the few things her father had kept that had any link to her mom. He'd gotten rid of everything else, angrily stating that she'd left him alone to raise their brat, so she didn't deserve to be remembered. But Abigail always suspected that he drank himself into a stupor every night looking at that picture. Because when she'd go in and see him, his face was always turned toward the photo.

Slowly, reluctantly, she allowed her eyes to make their way to her father's chair, which was in the exact place it had always been. She half expected to see him in the chair, glaring back at her. But he wasn't there. A sense of relief coursed through her, almost making her feel guilty. Almost.

She hadn't been allowed to go to his funeral, but someone had sent her the small write-up about it that had been in the Leaky Springs Gazette. She never knew who sent the article. She didn't really care. If someone had been trying to befriend her, they'd waited a little too long.

Abigail didn't inspect the old chair closely. She was sure the residue of his head still clung to and had become one with the dried, wrinkling leather. She'd take it outside and destroy it as soon as she could. She'd love to see it go up in flames, but she couldn't do anything to alert anyone that she was here. Not yet. She had to keep a very low profile.

Which meant she couldn't get the electricity or gas turned on. She'd even be afraid to try and use the old fireplace, since it had been unused for so long. She'd probably burn the house down if she tried to start a fire.

She slowly walked through the house and marveled at the flood of memories that overtook her. Marveled that all of them weren't bad. Again, Abigail realized that while her mom had been alive, she'd formed a few good memories. She didn't open the doors to her room or her dad's. Not yet. She wasn't quite ready to face those memories. She'd explore the kitchen first, and then she'd go face her room and hopefully be able to fix the bed to sleep on tonight.

She looked out the dingy kitchen window at the old barn. It still looked exactly like it had ten years ago. It had never been painted, so there was no dried, curling paint to distract from its rustic form. She remembered that last night, and how she'd been milking Betsy when—*Betsy! What happened to Betsy?*

Running from the house, Abigail headed for the barn. As she creaked open the door, she was engulfed with the musky scent of old hay, old wood, and dried cornhusks.

Her eyes adjusted to the inside light that seeped through cracks and knotholes as she made her way to the stall where they'd kept Betsy. The stall where she'd been milking Betsy that night.

Opening the door to the stall, Abigail stopped in mortified revulsion. There was her stool and milk pail, just where she'd left them. And curled around them were the skeletal remains of the old cow. She'd been left to starve to death. No one had rescued her. Probably no one even knew she was there.

Slumping slowly to the ground, Abigail Avery finally wept. She wept for the faithful old cow who had died alone and hungry. She wept for her mother who had died at such a young age. She wept for the little girl who had never known a normal childhood or young adulthood. And, finally, she wept for a father who had lost his way somewhere in life and had turned out to be a mean old drunk.

When she had cried until no more tears would fall,

Abigail realized darkness was settling around her. How long had she been out here? As she attempted to get up, strong hands encircled her upper arms and helped her to her feet.

Abigail screamed and fought the person who had helped her stand. Fought with all her might until the quiet, calming voice finally made its way into her consciousness enough for her to know that danger wasn't imminent.

She looked up into a face that held an expression she didn't recognize. If she had to put a name to it, even in this dimly lit barn, she'd say it was concern. Compassion? Surely not pity. She could tell his hair was blond and his eyes were green. And he looked, somehow, vaguely familiar.

She should be afraid, but her fear had subsided. She was in the land of enemies. She was sure she had no friends in this place. And yet she wasn't gazing into the eyes of an enemy. She was also sure of that.

"Abigail Avery—" his voice was like the caress of a soft Southern breeze. "The time for crying is over. It's time for you to rebuild your life."

Chapter 2

Outside the barn, the swiftly setting sun cast a red, eerie glow behind the cirrus clouds as Abigail looked up into the vaguely familiar face of the man who had just come to her aid. The niggling memory finally took on a name.

"Desh Elliot?" she asked.

"At your service," he said, sweeping low in an exaggerated bow.

"'Dashing Desh?'"

"Pardon me?"

"That's what all the girls in high school called you. 'Dashing Desh' Elliot."

A smile spread across his face. His bright green eyes danced with merriment as he swiped a large hand through his unruly blond hair. Twin dimples acted as periods to his beautiful smile.

"And did you call me 'Dashing Desh?'" His question sounded too personal to Abigail, who suddenly found herself on unfamiliar ground. For some reason her insides felt shaky.

Uncertain. A feeling she didn't like.

"All the silly girls called you that. You were, after all, the big captain of the football team. So they all swooned over you." She glanced at the sky. She had to get inside and get some things done before dark, since she wouldn't have any light to see by. "Look, Desh, I don't know how you found me here, but I'd really like to keep my return home a secret for a little while, if you don't mind."

"Did you?" he persisted, as if she hadn't said a word.

"I've got to go," she answered, turning from him.

His hand on her arm stopped her. His touch on her skin surprised her. Seared her. How many times had she sat on those hard, wooden bleachers at school and watched him practice his game? How many times had she imagined—fantasized—that he was looking up at her after each play he made? How many times had she reminded herself that Desh Elliot could have any girl he wanted, and he'd never come near white trash like her?

So what was he doing here now? Touching her? Looking at her with that look in his eyes?

"Okay, we'll go to the house together," he said, his hand still on her arm.

"No! You can't come in my house." She pulled her arm from him.

"Why not?"

"I told you! I have a lot of things to do before it gets dark." "Why before dark?" he asked, already knowing the answer.

"Desh—"

"I like 'Dashing Desh' better, if you don't mind." His green eyes danced in the dim light. Eyes that caught and held Abigail's against her will. Eyes that held something she had never felt directed toward her. Playfulness. Teasing. Almost—almost as if he were flirting with her. She'd seen movies in prison. She'd read books. And she'd heard the women talk. But she'd never experienced it personally. She had to be imagining that Desh Elliot was flirting with her. Just like she used to imagine he was watching her.

Mentally shaking herself back to the present, she explained, "Look, I don't have any electricity yet. I need to find some sheets and make up my bed before it gets dark. I need to find something to eat—" Her voice trailed off as she realized there would be nothing in the house to eat, and she hadn't even thought about that on her way out of town.

By now they were at the back door. Without waiting for an invitation, Desh stepped inside and flipped a switch that lit the kitchen. Abigail's eyes flew directly to the pot of steaming beef vegetable stew and pan of cornbread resting on a clean red-and-blue- checkered tablecloth. Place settings for two were waiting for them to sit and eat.

Apparently he'd set it up while she was in the barn. Which meant he'd been watching her. Knew when she arrived at the house. Knew she was in the barn. So where was his vehicle? Where had he been? Why hadn't she sensed that she was being watched? Uneasiness crept up her spine like a cold winter breeze.

Abigail's eyes went from the light bulb glowing overhead to the food, then back to Desh. "Why?" she asked, finally. "Why did you do this?" Questions inundated her. Questions that demanded answers. "How did you know I was coming home? And why would you care, anyway?"

The food's aroma found its way to Abigail, causing her stomach to knot and growl with hunger, reminding her that she hadn't eaten since breakfast. Her last prison meal.

Desh heard the rumblings inside her and led her to a chair. As she sat down and he pushed the chair in for her, she was almost certain she felt him touch her hair. She must be losing it! Coming home and finding him here was sending her over the edge of sanity.

"We have to talk, Abigail," he said, ladling out a large portion of stew on a plate and handing it to her.

Realizing that she was almost dizzy from hunger, Abigail took a spoonful of stew to her mouth. Heaven! The most expensive meal in the most exquisite restaurant in the world wouldn't have been any better than this stew.

"This is wonderful!" she exclaimed, momentarily forgetting about her questions.

"It's my specialty. I'm glad you like it," Desh answered.

"But why did you cook for me?"

"When you answer my one simple question, I'll answer all of yours," he said.

"What question?" she asked, looking genuinely confused.

"Did you call me 'Dashing Desh'?"

"You have a one-track mind, don't you?" She really didn't think she liked the way her chest was feeling. Tight. Like her heart was swelling, getting too large for her chest cavity. Was it fear? Or something else? Right now, it didn't feel like fear.

"I've been told that I do tend to get on one subject and ride it to death," he answered, his eyes doing a slow crawl over her face, pausing at her lips, her hair, and finally resting on her eyes. "So if you want answers, you have to go first."

"Oh, all right! Yes."

"Yes, what?"

Her eyes grew larger as she gazed back at him. He was actually going to make her say it. Normally her stubborn streak would have kicked in, but she sensed that he was more stubborn than she was, and she really wanted—needed—some answers.

"Yes, I called you 'Dashing Desh,'" she said, barely above a whisper.

"Want to know what I called you?" he drawled, watching her through half-closed eyes.

Was she imagining the tenderness in his voice? In his

eyes? "I can't believe you called me anything!" Abigail said in disbelief. "I can't believe you even knew I existed."

"I called you 'My Abigail.'"

Too stunned to speak, Abigail stared back at Desh. 'His Abigail'? *His* Abigail?

Watching the emotions play over her beautiful face, Desh wondered if he'd said too much, too soon. But he didn't care. He was not going to be silent any longer. He'd kept his feelings to himself when he was a kid, feeling the pressure of his peers. Knowing how everyone looked down on her and her family. Knowing what they would say if he followed his heart. Then one day it was too late to follow his heart. His heart was on its way to prison for a crime she didn't do.

He wouldn't wait any longer. Damn the peer pressure. Damn the wagging tongues. He'd spent the past ten years getting ready to protect, love and cherish her. The only reason he would go slowly now would be to keep from scaring her off. He didn't want her to think he was some kind of weirdo. A stalker or rapist.

Neither of them heard the gun until the bullet ripped into the pot of stew, sending a shred of the pot into the overhead light bulb, shattering glass and throwing the room into darkness.

"Get down!" Desh hissed. "Get on the floor!"

As Abigail obeyed his order he was on his feet, running to the back door.

"Desh, come back! Don't go out there!" The horror of another night flooded Abigail with vivid memories of finding her father dead and the blame being placed on her. What if they did that to Desh? Killed her and blamed it on him. She had to do something. She wouldn't just lie here and let them kill her, like they had done her father.

She was on her feet, ready to go after Desh, when she heard the slow squeak of the back door being opened. Someone was coming in! She flattened herself against the wall and held her breath.

"I think they're gone," Desh whispered, so close to her that his words fanned her hair, startling her. Causing her to expel her breath in a squeak.

Realizing she was okay, and standing close to him, Desh reached for her, pulling her hard against him. He expected her to fight him, but to his surprise she sank into him and rested her head on his shoulder. He gloried in feeling her soft, warm body pressed against his. Finally.

"They're going to kill me, just like they did my father, aren't they? But why? Why did they want my father dead? Why do they want me dead?"

"No! They aren't going to kill you!" Desh exploded. "They're going to try, but they're going to have to get through me to do it!"

Chapter 3

"**I want you to come home with me.** You can't stay in this house, now that they know someone was here."

"But how do they know I'm here?" Abigail asked, stepping away from the warm comfort of Desh's broad chest. She'd never known how comforting it was to be held close and protected by a man. She couldn't remember a man ever holding her this way. She didn't like the fact that it felt so good.

"Abigail, there's so much that I need to tell you. But I can't do it here. Come home with me. I have an extra bedroom where you can sleep."

"Where do you live?" Abigail had no intention of going home with Desh Elliot, but she did need any answers he might be able to give her.

"I bought the old Draper place after I got out of college. I'm in the process of renovating the old house. I have a lot to do on it, but I have two bedrooms, the living room and kitchen finished. And two bathrooms are usable."

"What do you need with a house that large?" Abigail

asked, remembering the huge two-story dwelling that had seemed so enormous to her when she was a child. Suddenly a thought struck her. "Desh, are you married?"

"No, not yet," he laughed.

"Not yet? Are you planning on getting married soon?"

"As soon as I can convince the woman of my dreams to have me," he answered. "So I need a big house. If she agrees, we may just have a house full of kids. Do you want kids, Abigail?"

The question brought Abigail back to reality with a harsh thud. Why were the two of them standing here in the dark discussing their future, when a potential killer might be outside lining up another shot?

"Desh, you need to leave! We can discuss all of this some other time. That hit-man may be out there getting ready to aim another shot at us while we stand here and talk about mundane things."

"Try hit-woman. I think I know who shot at us, and trust me, if she'd wanted to kill one of us, she would have. That shot was just a warning. I'm sure she's gone by now."

"Then it's okay to turn the lights on," Abigail said, starting toward the light switch.

"No!" Desh admonished, grabbing her before she could take another step. "No, Abigail. I said I *thought* I knew who fired the shot, and I *think* they're gone, but I'm not sure of it, so we can't take any chances. You simply cannot stay here tonight. Not until I do some more investigating on who fired that shot.

"Come on. Spend tonight at my house. Tomorrow I'll come back and see if I can find out who shot at us, and if I think it's safe, then you can come home."

Too tired to argue anymore, Abigail allowed Desh to lead her through the back door. She'd come back tomorrow. She had to get to the bottom of this. This was her house and she didn't plan on being driven away from it. Not again. There were a lot of people who were about to have to answer to Abigail Avery. Tomorrow was a good day to start.

They were halfway to the barn before Abigail realized where they were headed. Darkness had settled in with a vengeance, and the barn was just a darker shadow in the murky night.

Desh must have parked his vehicle behind the barn so she wouldn't see it, she reasoned. But when he passed the building and continued to walk toward the dense woods that spread out behind the barn, Abigail realized there was no vehicle. They were headed into the thick forest that she'd always been so afraid of when she was a child. Afraid to go "in there," because her father had told her that monsters were in those woods and would eat her alive if she went past a certain place. And in later years, when she was too old for the monster stories, he'd told her if she went past a certain tree, horrible things would happen to her. She'd never questioned her father as to what horrible things. She hadn't questioned him, because to question him was to invite his wrath.

Afraid. Abigail realized that fear had gripped her. Numbed her. Why was Desh leading her into the woods? She stopped suddenly and snatched her hand from his grip.

"What are you doing?" she demanded. "Why are we going in there?"

The moon slid from behind the thunderhead that had been concealing it. The sudden moonlight illuminated Desh's face, giving it an eerie glow. His green eyes reflected the light, and just then a strong gust of wind stood his blond hair straight up, giving him a wild, almost demented look.

Abigail popped her hand over her mouth to stifle the scream that was threatening to tear its way through her throat. She turned and started running back toward the house they'd just left. But before she'd taken over ten steps, she felt Desh grab her shoulders and force her to the ground. She fought him frantically, trying to break free of the strong arms that pinned her down.

"Abigail! What is wrong with you?" Desh whooshed as one of her elbows caught him in the stomach. Finally capturing both of her hands and holding them behind her head, he threw a leg over hers and drew in a ragged breath when she finally stopped her struggle.

"What is wrong with you?" he repeated, peering down into her beautiful moonlit face. Her glorious red hair—that hair that he'd dreamed about every night—was splayed on the ground around her head. How he'd love to freeze time right now. Freeze this picture of her. Except the fear in her eyes. Fear of him?

"Abigail? Tell me what's wrong. What frightened you? Did I do something?"

Abigail looked up into Desh's face. The moonlight now seemed to soften his features, bringing back memories of the Dashing Desh she'd known in school. Her heart rate started to slow, but not totally. He was, after all, holding her down, and she still didn't know his intentions. But he didn't look threatening anymore. Maybe she'd overreacted. Maybe the stress of all the happenings of the day had frayed her nerve endings.

"Why were we going into the woods?" she asked. "I've been afraid of those woods all my life, so I panicked when we started in there."

Slowly, testing to see how she was going to react, Desh released Abigail's hands. Although having her pinned to the ground like this was sending all kinds of erotic thoughts charging through his mind, and his body was quickly reacting to those thoughts. He'd better get them under control, right now.

"Don't you know?" he asked, propping up on an elbow while he continued to gaze down at her. He was relieved when she sat up but didn't try to run away again.

"Know what?" Abigail brushed her hands across the cool grass. It had been so many years since she'd sat in the grass and felt its lush texture against her skin. Free! She was free! The thought crashed through her mind so hard her body jerked.

Desh grabbed her arm. "Don't bolt on me again, Abigail."

"Know what?" she repeated her question.

"Don't you know what's inside that thick grove of trees? You've lived here all your life. Surely you know."

"My dad told me that if I went in those woods something terrible would happen to me." She was almost embarrassed to admit the fear that had been instilled in her was still present after all these years.

"Don't you know about the caves that are under most of this territory around here? Don't you know about the huge cavern that runs under your property?"

"I remember hearing some of the kids talk about caves when I was in school, but no, I didn't know there were any under my property." Just the thought that they might be sitting over some huge hole made Abigail uncomfortable. She guessed it made sense that there might be caves around, though. After all, Leaky Springs sat almost on the east Alabama line, and there were close to three thousand caves in Alabama.

"So—you don't know what your old man did for a living?"

"He said he got a check from the government because of a war wound," Abigail answered.

"That may be true, but he was also a bootlegger! He made enough moonshine whiskey to keep this entire county drunk on the weekends."

"Well, I'm not surprised at anything he did," Abigail said, "but what did he do with the money? Mom and I never saw any of it. But back to the caves. Are you saying that's what's on the other side of those trees? Is that why he didn't want me in there?"

Before Desh could answer the moon was covered by another ominous cloud. Lightning sent a spiraling display of fireworks across the distant sky. A muted rumble of thunder followed.

"We'd better get on our way to my house, or we're going to get wet," Desh said, rising and offering Abigail a helping hand.

"Don't be afraid, Abigail," he added, as he led her toward the foreboding stand of trees. "I wouldn't put you in harm's way. I promise you I'll always do whatever it takes to protect you."

Abigail wanted to spend time thinking over the promise he'd just made her, but was too busy watching the mass of trees they were swiftly heading into.

Thick darkness engulfed them as Desh led her through a dense patch of undergrowth. He made sure the low tree branches didn't switch back and hit her as he led the way deeper and deeper into the blackness. The loud pounding of Abigail's heart muted all other sounds.

Suddenly the undergrowth cleared. There were no limbs swishing around Abigail's body. There was nothing but the blackest blackness she'd ever experienced. The darkness was so complete that she felt dizzy. Disoriented. Confused at the emptiness surrounding her. Almost as if she were about to fall headlong into a hole.

"Desh!" she screeched.

"You're okay, Abigail," he answered, as light suddenly replaced the blackness.

Abigail was relieved to see the large flashlight clutched in his hand. But she was amazed at what the light revealed. Straight ahead of them lay a long tunnel. Apparently a natural tunnel, as rocks and dirt formed the walls.

Returning her gaze to Desh, she realized he was watching

her.

"What is this?" she asked, almost afraid of his answer.

"This is one of the many reasons your old man didn't want you in these woods. He was afraid you'd stumble onto one of the caves. And he was right. You could have gotten lost, and something terrible could have happened to you. Or you could have found his whiskey still and exposed his little operation."

"But I thought we were going to your house. What does this cave have to do with going to your house?" The hair on the back of her neck prickled a little. What was Desh up to? After all, she didn't know anything about this guy.

"I know you're tired, but we can walk to my house through this tunnel. It's about a quarter of a mile. I discovered this passageway accidentally, after I'd been in the Draper house for a while. This is the way I got to your house today. It's shorter than going by the road. Come on." He took her hand and led her deeper into the damp corridor ahead of them.

Abigail was seized with apprehension. Should she follow this man into a hole in the ground, or should she turn and run, and take the chance of spending the night in her own home?

Sensing her fear, Desh stopped and turned to her. He took a small derringer from his pants pocket, turned her hand palm up and placed the gun in it.

"If it will make you feel better, you hold on to this until we get to my house. Before long, Abigail, you'll know that I'm on your side. I'm not your enemy." Turning, he continued to lead her through the tunnel.

Abigail wanted to hand the small pistol back to Desh, but the feel of the smooth steel against her skin seemed to give her some comfort in these unfamiliar surroundings. She wasn't afraid of Desh. It was just that this entire day had been very unsettling. So she held on to the gun, making sure it was pointed toward the ground at all times, and allowed Desh to lead her on.

At one point he stopped and pointed to what appeared to be a small open room and turned the flashlight upwards. Bats clustered and hung from the ceiling. Some of them were moving restlessly. She recoiled at the sight, so Desh continued to walk past the opening. But Abigail felt chills creep up her spine. She expected to feel the sharp teeth of one of the bats sink into her flesh at any moment.

"They're getting ready to fly from the cave and look for food," Desh said, leading her on.

Weariness engulfed her. She didn't think she could take another step. She was about to tell Desh that she couldn't go any further when she thought she saw the end of the tunnel ahead of them. On looking closer, she realized she was seeing a wall of rock with no opening. A dead end. So what now?

Again, a little niggling of fear flitted up her spine. But just before it settled in, Desh reached into a cranny in the rocks and pulled a six-rung ladder over in front of him. He climbed up a few rungs, then reached over his head and pushed a wooden door open. The space was square and large enough for them to pass through. He made his way up the ladder first, then motioned for her to come up. When she stood beside him, he pulled the ladder up and closed the wooden door.

"This way, nobody can get in here if they should accidentally find the tunnel," he explained.

As Abigail stepped out of his way so he could stand the ladder against the wall, she realized she was inside a building. The room was lined with shelves, which seemed to be filled with canned goods and other items.

"This is my cellar," Desh explained.

"Your cellar? Why is there a tunnel running from your cellar to my property?" she asked. How many more mysteries could she go through in one day? Her head was already spinning from all that had happened.

"As I said, I found it accidentally. I was cleaning out the

cellar one day, and moved that old trunk." He pointed to a huge weathered trunk that stood against the wall. "And when I did, I realized that I'd uncovered a trap door. Naturally, I had to explore where it went, and that's when I discovered that it led to your property. This house was built in the 1800s, so the initial builder probably meant to use the tunnel as an escape route if he ever needed it.

"Your house is a newer house, so I don't think the tunnel between the two was deliberate. It was probably just a coincidence."

Hearing Abigail's tired sigh, Desh said, "Why don't we get some sleep and I'll take you exploring tomorrow." He headed for a stone stairway that led to another wooden door.

As curious as Abigail was, sleep seemed like something she hadn't done in a long, long time. So without arguing, she followed Desh up the stairway and through the heavy wooden door. She was amazed when they stepped into a very modern kitchen.

Desh locked the door that led from the cellar, then flipped a light switch that flooded the dimly lit kitchen with bright light.

"Okay, before I tuck you in for the night," he said, giving Abigail a wicked smile, "let's see if we can finish that dinner we started. I saved some of that stew and cornbread for me, but we can eat it now. I'll pour us a glass of milk."

He pulled out a chair and motioned for her to sit down at the small table in the kitchen. After she was seated, he busied himself putting food on the table, then sat down close beside her.

"Here, you'd better take this back," she said, handing him the gun.

"Would it make you feel better to hang on to it?"

"No. But thanks, anyway." The fact that he'd offered made her feel she could trust him.

The food was even better than it had been the first time Abigail had tried to eat it. Maybe because she was even hungrier now than she was then.

They ate in silence for a few minutes before Desh spoke. "I've waited a long time for the day Abigail Avery would sit at my table and share a meal with me." His eyes were warm with that *thing* that made Abigail uncomfortable. That thing she wasn't familiar with. That feeling in the pit of her being.

Sensing her discomfort, Desh continued, "We've got a lot of talking to do, Abigail. I have a lot of explaining to do, too. But it can wait. I know you're tired, so finish your meal and I'll take you to your room. Tomorrow is another day. You're free now. We have a lot of wonderful days ahead of us to talk."

Abigail didn't know anything could feel as heavenly as the bed she lay in a little while later. She'd slept so many nights on the cot in prison that she'd forgotten what it felt like to stretch her legs out in all directions and not have them fall off the side of the bed. She'd forgotten how soft a good pillow could feel. And how good it could smell after the pillowcase had dried on a clothesline out in the open air.

After Desh had brought her to the room, she'd taken a shower, dressed in an old cotton gown that he'd found some-where—she didn't ask where, but she suspected it had been Molly Draper's—and now she felt like a queen in a castle, so far removed was she from the prison where she'd spent the night only twenty-four hours ago.

She glanced around the room again. The new wallpaper complemented the time period of the old house, but still had a fresh, modern look. The furniture was antique, but well taken care of. Everything looked beautiful, but the thing that touched her most was the nightlight with an angel cover that burned dimly from a wall socket. Desh had explained that he wanted her to be able to see her surroundings in case she woke up during the night and forgot where she was.

As sleep threatened to claim her, she promised herself that tomorrow she must find out why Desh Elliot was taking such good care of her. How he knew so much about her. And why he hadn't answered her question when she'd asked how anyone knew she was home.

Chapter 4

The hand in her hair brought Abigail abruptly awake. "No! I told you no!" she shouted, pushing the hand away and bolting to a sitting position.

But the face she stared into wasn't Josey Jones. And she remembered instantly that she wasn't still in prison.

"Abigail! I'm sorry! Settle down. I'm not going to hurt you," Desh tried to assure her.

"What are you doing in here?" she asked. Sleep still claimed half of her brain, but she was awake enough to detect the wonderful aroma of coffee.

"I brought you breakfast in bed. I thought it would be a good way to celebrate your first morning out of prison."

"I've never had breakfast in bed," she said, watching as he placed a bed tray over her lap.

"I've never served breakfast in bed to a beautiful woman, so this is a first for both of us," Desh answered, as he sat in a chair beside the bed and placed a tray on his lap. "Now. We'll have breakfast together."

Abigail looked from the tray of eggs, bacon, hash-browns, biscuits and gravy back to Desh. Why? Why was he being so nice to her? She'd never had a man be nice to her, and she wasn't sure how to react. Wasn't sure if she liked the feelings that churned inside her. Feelings that seemed to accompany Desh Elliot when he was around.

"Abigail, who did you think I was, just now? Who has tried to hurt you? To take advantage of you?"

Abigail took a tentative sip of the hot coffee. It was heavenly. Coffee in the prison had been horrible. But this—this was wonderful. Should she tell him about Josey and prison existence? Was she ready to share that part of her life with anyone?

"Abigail?" The persistent note in his voice convinced her that stalling wouldn't help. Straight honesty was all that Desh Elliot would accept, something told her.

"There was a—a—" Embarrassment halted her voice. "There was this person in prison—"

"Did one of the guards force himself on you? I'll kill the son-of-a-bitch!" Desh's outburst startled Abigail out of her timidity.

"No! It was a woman! She wanted me to be her lover. But I convinced her that she was after the wrong person," Abigail ended shakily.

She watched Desh visibly relax and lean back in his chair. A slight smile tugged at the corners of his mouth. "I'll just bet you did," he said. "Not that I could blame anyone—man or woman—for lusting after your beautiful body." His glance rested on the bulges her breasts created under the frumpy old gown she wore. The tray had pulled the material taut across her chest, leaving little to the imagination. And apparently Desh had an active imagination.

Horrified at what she saw when she followed the direction of his eyes, Abigail immediately tried to pull the sheet up to cover herself.

"Don't be ashamed of your beauty, Abigail," Desh said, placing his hand on hers to stop her efforts. "Don't ever be ashamed of your beauty. Don't run from it. You *are* a beautiful woman."

Abigail had known ridicule in her life. She'd felt anger directed toward her. She'd sensed people looking down on her. She remembered a time when her mother didn't seem to mind having her around, but her mother had never complimented her on anything. So Abigail Avery didn't know what a compliment was supposed to feel like. Couldn't remember anyone complimenting her on anything.

And she definitely had never had a man compliment her. Beautiful? The thought made her almost laugh out loud. Her beautiful? Not in a million years! Desh Elliot was either blind or just plain weird. But he didn't look to be either as he sat and watched Abigail digest what he'd just said.

A big smile spread across her face as she lifted her eyes from the hand that covered hers to look at him.

"Desh, you really need to have your eyes checked," she said. "Apparently, you aren't seeing too well if you can call me beautiful."

"No, Abigail. My vision is perfect 20/20. And I'm looking at the most beautiful woman in the world. And before I'm finished, I'm going to convince you of that. Now, if we don't eat this breakfast, it's going to get cold."

She pulled her eyes from his, even more confused now. He seemed so sincere. Seemed so intent on making her feel— what? What were these feelings? When she had time to think about them, she *really* had to explore what was going on here.

The distant crowing of a rooster reminded Abigail where she was. The old Draper place, as people had always called it. If memory served her, the house sat at the end of the road. Then why had she heard trucks passing on and off during the night?

"Desh, has the road been extended past this place? I remember that the house was at the end of the road and there was no through traffic."

"It's still a dead end," Desh said, as he began eating the food on his plate.

"Then why did I hear what sounded like big trucks passing by during the night?"

"What?"

"I was awakened at least three times by what sounded like a big truck—maybe a dump truck—in the distance."

"Abigail, that's impossible. There's no way a big truck, or any other vehicle, has passed here during the night. My pickup is the only one that's been on the road to this house in a long time. Sometimes someone who doesn't know it's a dead end will come almost to the house, but they usually turn around down at the mailbox once they realize what they've done. Maybe you were just dreaming."

"No, I wasn't dreaming. Truck engines woke me up."

"And you're sure you weren't just dreaming or remembering sounds from prison? It's going to take you a few days to adjust to being out of there. Maybe your brain was having flashbacks."

"Maybe so," Abigail said, now doubting that she'd actually heard anything. Desh seemed so sure that it couldn't have been trucks, so who was she to argue with him?

"Are you finished?" he asked, indicating her half-eaten breakfast.

"Yes. It was wonderful. Prison food wasn't that bad, but this was heaven in comparison."

"Well, it must not have been that wonderful. You didn't eat it all," he teased.

"I'm not a lumber-jack! That was enough food to feed two people," she argued.

"When you're dressed, come downstairs to the living room and we'll talk about the day ahead of us."

"My day ahead will be me going home and trying to figure out how to proceed with my life. I don't see a lot of discussion to be done about that," Abigail said.

Taking the trays and heading for the door, Desh turned back to her. "I'll see you in a little while," he said, and left the room.

"Stubborn man!" Abigail said, and heard him chuckle as he headed down the hallway.

It didn't take Abigail long to shower and dress. She had a mental list of questions she wanted to ask Desh Elliot this morning.

She made her way downstairs then followed a hallway barren of any décor. Abigail imagined it lined with family portraits. Desh did say he was remodeling, though. Would he want family portraits on his walls? But what did it matter to her? She couldn't care less what he wanted, she reminded herself.

She followed the sounds of soft music until she came to a huge parlor she assumed was the "living room" Desh had referred to. Desh wasn't in the room, but Abigail was intrigued with the classical music wafting around her. Classical music? Desh Elliot was full of surprises. If she'd thought about it, she'd have imagined him listening to country music.

As she stood in the middle of the large room, faint, distant memories sifted through her mind. Memories of being in this room and listening to her mom and another woman—was it Molly Draper?—talk about something. The "something" nagged at her brain as if it wanted to surface. What? She'd forgotten about ever being in this house, much less hearing something that she should remember.

"Here you are," Desh said as he entered the room from an outside door. "It's a decent morning, would you like to sit on the front porch? It's not as humid as it has been."

Why did his voice remind her of slow sunny days and quiet rainy nights all rolled up in the same package? Abigail wondered. Why did his slow Southern drawl affect her at all? She'd grown up in the South, for goodness sakes! But his drawl was different. It was a cultured drawl. His words were pronounced correctly. His English was perfect, and his enunciation was immaculate. It was just the way his tongue curled around the words and gave them that sensual sound that made her weak all over—

Whoa! Where had that come from? Stunned at her thoughts, Abigail tried to snap herself back to the present. "Sure!" she exclaimed, too quickly.

"Abigail? Are you okay? Is something troubling you?"

Reaching for anything to get her mind off of her previous thoughts, Abigail said, "I'm fine. It's just that being in this room is bringing back some memories that I didn't even know I had," she answered. *And making me think things that I shouldn't be thinking,* she thought.

"What do you mean?"

"Well, I'm remembering being in this room, and up until today, I didn't remember that I'd ever been in this house. It was just always the 'old Draper place,' like everyone referred to it."

"So—you didn't visit here when you were a child?"

"No. My parents didn't visit anyone."

"Are you telling me that you don't know who the Drapers were?"

"All I know is that they were an older couple who lived here. I never knew anything else about them."

"Abigail, Jim and Molly Draper were your mom's parents. They were your grandparents."

"*What?*"

"Jim and Molly disowned your mom after she married your dad. The story has it that they couldn't stand the thought of their only child being married to a loser like him. I'm sorry to be the one to break this to you. I thought you already knew the story."

Suddenly the nagging memory broke through. Her mom, Molly, and a man yelling at each other. Her mom and Molly crying, but the man standing firm in what he was saying. She couldn't remember what he was saying, but in her faint child's memory he was arguing against the two women.

"So you never got to know your grandparents?" Desh continued. "I thought it was odd you didn't have any reaction to the fact that I'd bought your grandparents' home.

"I can understand them not wanting to associate with your dad. And I might be able to understand them not wanting to have anything to do with their daughter if she insisted on marrying him. But I sure can't understand them not wanting to get to know you. Their own grandchild."

"Desh, are you sure you have your facts straight? I mean, I just can't believe that I lived this close to my grandparents and never knew it. What kind of sheltered world did I grow up in?"

"You grew up with an abusive alcoholic father and an enabling, weak mother who was unlucky enough to fall in love with the wrong man. Sometimes kids from families like that do grow up in sheltered environments. They're told to keep family matters quiet because it's none of anyone else's business. Fear is instilled in them to keep things to themselves."

"Yes. I know all about that. Fear was my playmate."

"My precious little Abigail." His voice was so quiet, she wasn't sure she heard the words correctly. "Wait right here. I have something to show you."

When Desh returned to the room, he held a tattered cardboard box that looked like a faded shoebox. He placed it on the table and opened it. It contained a few yellowed, black and white photos. He pulled one out and handed it to Abigail. "Who does that look like?" he asked.

Abigail studied the faded photograph. Her mind wouldn't wrap around the time warp the photo created. It seemed to be a picture of her, dressed in clothes from a time gone by. But she'd never had a photo like this taken. Puzzled, she looked up at Desh, who watched her closely.

"That's Molly Draper when she was about the age you are now. When I found this old box of pictures, I couldn't believe how much you look like her. Of course, she was larger in this picture than I remembered you. Than you were when you left here. But the hair . . . I could tell even in this faded black and white photo that she had your wonderful hair." He stopped and spent a moment gazing at Abigail's hair.

"These are yours," he said, putting the lid back on the box and handing it to her.

Abigail clutched the box to her chest. She couldn't wait to explore the contents. Maybe there would be pictures of her mom as a little girl. But how would she know who these people were? She wouldn't recognize them. But it didn't matter. This box was like a link to her past. A past that she'd known so little about.

She turned slowly and took in the room. This room should hold warm memories for her. Memories of Christmas and Thanksgiving gatherings. Memories of laughter. Of times spent with loving grandparents. She should be familiar with the entire house. Should know every nook and corner. Should know where the favorite hiding place of a little girl would be. Instead, she was a stranger in this house, just as she'd always felt like a stranger in everything she did. A stranger in this very world she walked through.

Feeling more alone than she ever had, tears spilled down her cheeks. She had been so close to happiness, yet never knew it existed.

Strong arms circled her and pulled her close. When she tried to resist, Desh held her tighter. "Abigail Avery, you aren't alone in this world anymore," he said, as if reading her mind. "I'm here to be by your side as long as you'll let me. I want to help you through the upcoming months. I want to be here for you to lean on. Lean on me, Abigail. Don't be afraid to let me help you."

His soft, murmured words of comfort strengthened Abigail. Reminded her of why she'd come home. Reminded her of what she had to do.

"Why, Desh? What's in it for you?" she asked, stepping back from him.

Chapter 5

"Let's just say I don't like injustice. And you, Abigail, were victim of a great injustice."

"Desh! What do you know? Tell me! I've waited ten years to get back here and find out what happened that night with my father, and why I was framed for his murder. What do you know?" Excitement churned inside Abigail.

"I've been gathering some clues about your situation, but I still don't have anything provable. Mostly suspicions, backed up by a few facts. But with you here to fill me in on some things, I think we can get to the bottom of who set you up. And I don't think the 'why' will be that hard either." Desh walked to the window and stared into space, trying to decide just how much to tell Abigail at this early point.

"Look," he continued, turning back to her, "why don't we concentrate on figuring out a disguise for you. You said you don't want anyone to know you're back yet. I think that's a great idea. So we've got to disguise you."

"Judge Haney didn't recognize me yesterday," she said.

"That's true, but sooner or later someone is going to recognize you."

"Desh, how did you know I was back?"

The question he'd hoped she wouldn't ask. How much should he tell her? If he told her everything . . . Should he keep it business or on a personal level? He decided to go with the latter, hoping again that she wouldn't think he was some kind of pervert.

"Abigail, I've already told you that I called you 'my Abigail' when we were kids. I think I had a crush on you all of my school years. I don't know why. Part of it was because of that lost, sad look that was always in your eyes. I wanted so badly to see you smile. Part of it was because you never played with the other kids. You just sat and watched the fun go on around you. But most of it was because of that mass of red hair that turns to pure gold in the sunlight.

"I stood and watched the day they put you in that police car and took you away. The last thing I saw was Sheriff Lucas' big hand on your beautiful hair as he shoved you into the car. I wanted to kill him for touching you.

"I was looking out of my—an office window in the courthouse yesterday when you stepped off the bus. When I saw the wind lift and whirl your hair up in the air, my heart stood still. I knew my Abigail had come home." There. He'd said it. The truth. Only part of the truth, but the truth.

Stunned silence filled the room. Abigail didn't know how to respond to the things he'd just said. They were so foreign to her on every level that words escaped her. She went to the closest chair and shakily sat down.

"So—" Desh interrupted the silence. "I don't think anyone will recognize your body. It's changed a lot since you left here. And I do mean a lot!" A wicked smile spread across his face as he looked Abigail up and down.

"Desh!"

"Sorry. But the change is wonderful, Abigail. You can't blame a man for looking," he said. "Anyway, it's the hair we've got to disguise."

"Then I'll cut it," Abigail quickly volunteered.

"That won't change the color. Would you consider dying it, just until we finish our investigation?"

"I'll do whatever it takes to get to the bottom of this thing. So, what color? Black? Blonde?"

"Why don't we go blonde, that seems to be the popular color these days. Who are you going to be? You're obviously new in town, so who are you and why are you here?"

"I told Judge Haney that I was here checking on some real estate. He didn't seem to like that idea. Said there wasn't anything for sale around here."

"Oh, I'll bet he didn't like that idea," Desh chuckled. "Hmmm. Checking on real estate. That's going to raise a lot of suspicion, but since you've already told him that, we probably need to stick with the story."

"Why would my looking for real estate raise suspicions?"

"Because everything that comes up for sale around here is immediately sucked up by the good old boys running this town. They're trying to buy up everything around in order to control this area. So they'll be very suspicious of a stranger coming in wanting to buy property. But maybe a little suspicion will throw them off track of who you really are. This may be the perfect way to go."

"Is that why I kept getting letters wanting to buy my place?"

"Yes. They really want your property."

"But why? The place is worthless!"

"Well—it depends on what they want to use it for. That's the mystery I can't quite figure out, but I believe it has something to do with the caves that run under your place and this one. I think the major, larger rooms of the caves lie under your property. If these people were normal townspeople, I'd think they want to build some kind of tourist attraction. But these good old boys don't want anyone new in this area. Hell, they don't want some of us who grew up here to stay. So—"

"How did you manage to buy this house if they're buying everything? Especially if they know the caves connect the two properties?"

"I don't think they know the caves connect, yet. I think that's why they haven't started to harass me about wanting this property."

"So where do we start?" It appeared that she had a partner whether she wanted him or not. But suddenly that didn't seem like such a bad idea. Maybe with Desh's help her progress would be faster. He'd been here all the years she'd been away, so he had more knowledge of what was going on than she did.

"I think we should start by getting your hair taken care of. Do you remember Mabelle Henley from school?"

"A petite, quiet girl with big brown eyes and curly brown hair?"

"Yes. Well, Mabelle is the local beautician—or hair stylist, as she prefers to be called. I think we can trust her, even if she figures out who you are. She hates Judge Haney with a real passion, for some reason. And doesn't try too hard to keep her feelings about him quiet. I'll call her and see if we can set up a private appointment. That way none of the gossipy old town biddies will be talking about that new redhead in town who got her beautiful hair bleached out."

As Desh went immediately to the phone to make the call, Abigail pondered how easily he referred to her "beautiful" hair, and how complimentary he was toward her.

Why would someone like Desh Elliot ever be interested in her? It just didn't make sense. And why was he so eager to help her? Did he, too, have ulterior motives? Maybe trusting him to help her wasn't such a good idea. But it did seem like the best way right now. She'd just be careful and watch him. If, at any time, she felt threatened by him, he'd be out of her life.

"Okay," Desh said, coming back to her. "We have an appointment at eight o'clock tonight. It'll be dark by then, so we should be able to go in the back door of Mabelle's salon without being seen. She wanted to know who you are and why all the secrecy. I told her you're running away from an abusive husband and want to stay here in town for awhile under the guise of a real estate agent, and you need to change your appearance just in case the jerk comes looking for you."

"You have quite the imagination, don't you?"

"Well, in my line of business, it's always good to come up with a story fast," he answered.

"And what is your line of business?" Abigail asked.

"I'm a lawyer," he answered.

"Dashing Desh Elliot, a lawyer?" Amusement pulled the corners of Abigail's lips up almost into a smile. "That's the last thing I'd ever have imagined you to be."

"And what did you imagine me to be?" he asked, suddenly hopeful that she'd ever given him any thought at all.

"So—while we wait to get my hair done, we have an entire day ahead of us. I'm going to go to my house and look around," Abigail said, changing the subject abruptly.

"Oh no, you don't. You're not getting off the hook that easily. What did you imagine me to be?" Desh persisted.

"I always imagined that you'd be some hot-shot football coach since you were so good at the game and since your dad was a teacher and the principal of the school." She didn't dare tell him of the brief fantasies she'd allowed herself. Of being married to him, having his kids, and him being head coach at the school. Fantasies of being part of the community in a normal setting. Of even being respected because she was married to an upstanding person like Desh Elliot. Remembering the absurd fantasy and how impossible something like that could have been brought a poignant smile to her full lips.

"Actually, I did consider that. But—things happened that changed my mind." No need to tell her yet that he'd decided to become a lawyer in order to eventually try and convict the guilty bastards who had railroaded her to prison.

Standing, Abigail said, "I'm going to the house to check things out."

"Abigail, after last night's shooting, I don't think that's a good idea. I want to go back and look around to see if my suspicions are correct as to who did the shooting. But I don't think it's safe for you to be there."

"Desh. I'm going to the house today. I didn't spend ten years waiting to get out of prison just to come home and hide out from unsafe situations. Now, with you or without you, I'm going."

"Okay, we'll go back through the caves. Meet me in the kitchen in fifteen minutes," he reluctantly agreed. Damn! His quiet little Abigail had developed a major backbone while she was in prison.

Desh brought a larger flashlight than he'd had last night, so Abigail could see and appreciate more of the cave's surroundings. They passed stalactites that hung from the cave ceiling like huge icicles. Stalagmites adorned the floor, as if some ancient cave dweller had carved ice sculptures and left them there to be appreciated by later generations. At one point Desh stopped and shined the light in a corner where a small pool glistened with clear, pristine water.

Abigail was in awe that this beauty, this underworld, had been right at her fingertips all of her life, and she'd never known it.

As they left the cave and came to the edge of the woods, Desh placed his hand on her arm to stop her. Carefully he surveyed the house and barn, watching for any sign of movement, to make sure nobody was on the place except them.

Cautiously, still holding her arm, he moved forward, staying in the shade of the barn, where, once again, he paused and watched the house closely.

"Everything looks quiet, so I guess it's okay for you to look around in the house. I'm going to see if I can find any clues as to who shot at us."

As Abigail started to move away from him, Desh cautioned, "If you hear or see anything suspicious, get out of there immediately. Go back to the cave. We'll meet there if anybody shows up here, okay?"

"Okay," Abigail agreed. Something in Desh's voice sent chills crawling up her spine. He was being way too cautious. What did he know that he hadn't told her?

The door hinge whined loudly as Abigail stepped inside the screened back porch. In the light of day she could see that things were just as they'd been left ten years ago.

Cobwebs covered the "outside" boots she'd worn in the wintertime. They sat exactly where she'd left them the last time she'd worn them. An old straightback chair held a pan of what was once some vegetable—she didn't remember what—that had turned into a cracked cake of unrecognizable matter. The handmade table was cluttered with dust-covered fruit jars.

Walking into the kitchen, Abigail remembered the panic she'd felt last night when the bullet had zinged past her head. She looked around at the mess the broken bowl had spilled onto the table and floor. She'd have to clean that up, but first she wanted to explore the rest of the house.

At first glance, her room seemed just like the back porch—frozen in time for ten years. Then she noticed a piece of clothing hanging out of one of the chests of drawers.

She hadn't left anything hanging out of a drawer. That was one of the things that would have brought the wrath of her father down on her. He'd inspected her room every morning to make sure it was spotless. She'd learned early in life to make sure nothing was out of place.

She went to the drawer—her underwear drawer, she'd called it—pulled it out, and sucked in her breath. Everything was clumped and shoved around, as if someone had searched through it. She quickly snatched open the rest of the drawers only to find that each one of them had been scrambled through. She hadn't left them like this. Everything had to be folded and in its place.

She found the same pattern in her closet. All her clothes— oh! how she hated those drab clothes her dad insisted she wear—had been shuffled and pilfered through. Even her shoes lay in disarray.

She quickly made her way to her dad's room and stood in amazement. The room was in shambles. Every item that had ever been on a shelf or in a drawer lay scattered on the floor. The mattress was ripped to shreds.

Someone had been desperately searching for something. But what? What could her dad possibly have had that was of interest to anyone? This didn't make any sense. They were dirt poor. They had nothing!

"Abigail?" Desh's voice preceded him through the house. "Are you still—?" He stopped when he spotted her and the look on her face. "What? What's wrong?" he asked, coming up beside her. "Oh, my!" he said, looking at the junked room.

"What could anyone possibly think they'd find?" Abigail asked again.

"The deed to the property, would be my guess," Desh answered.

"Oh. That does make sense. Do you think they found it?"

"No."

"How can you sound so sure?"

"When did you get the last letter asking you to sell?"

"Just before I got out of prison."

"If they had the deed, I don't think they'd still be trying to contact you," he reasoned.

"But maybe they did this yesterday."

"Did you check this room yesterday, when you got here?"

"No, I didn't check in here, or in my bedroom. I was going to, but when I thought about Betsy, I ran to the barn. I don't know why. Common sense should have told me that she wouldn't still be there—except she was." Sadness filled her voice.

"Have you checked your bedroom, yet?"

"Yes. It's been searched. Not trashed like this, but my clothes have been gone through."

"Dirty bastards," Desh mumbled as he headed to her room.

Abigail stood at the door and watched Desh open each drawer and look at the tumbled disarray. Embarrassment churned inside her as she watched him take note of the things that had once been so personal to her. Things that now seemed so sad and depressing.

"This wasn't done yesterday," he said, after glancing through her closet.

"How do you know that?"

"Because dust has collected on these hanging garments. If they'd been searched yesterday or last night, dust wouldn't have had time to settle on them."

"So they didn't find what they were looking for."

"No. Which is probably why we were shot at last night. Someone might have thought that we were here doing our own search."

"Do you think the person who shot at us knew it was you in the house?"

"I don't think so. From the evidence I just found, someone

has been watching the house, which I've suspected for some time now. There was a spot where someone has been hanging out. Maybe more than one person, but the footsteps I saw were of the same person, wearing the same pair of shoes. Someone with small feet."

"Well, you're just Mr. Sherlock Holmes, aren't you!" Abigail joked, in spite of the tinge of fear that clutched at her heart.

"I'm learning to be. It just might save our lives," he said, then regretting his openness after seeing the flash of fear in her eyes. But maybe a little fear might make her take him more seriously about not staying in this house.

"What do you mean, 'save our lives'?" Abigail questioned. "Do you really think we're in danger?"

"If the person who shot at us is who I think it is, we could be in a lot of danger. I don't think she would blink an eye at killing someone."

"She?" Abigail squeaked.

"Yes, 'she.' She's already been on trial for killing her ex-husband. But the case got thrown out due to lack of proof."

"Who is she?"

"The good judge's wife. *The* Mrs. Harry Haney, as she likes to introduce herself. It seems she and the judge were having an affair when her husband 'accidentally' shot himself three times in the head.

"Rumor has it that she and her husband belonged to a militia group before moving to this area. The same rumor says she's an excellent marksman. I suspected last night that she was the one who shot at us. That's why I said it was just a warning. And today, I'm 99.9 percent sure it was her."

"What makes you so sure?"

"The shoe prints. The prints are small, and they're high-heeled shoes. Mrs. Harry Haney doesn't go anywhere without wearing her heels."

Chapter 6

The back of the building was secluded from anyone's view, Abigail observed as Desh parked his truck behind Mabelle's Hair Salon. A dim light was barely visible through a small window.

Well, here goes my makeover, she thought as she and Desh made their way to the back door. Apprehension curled in the pit of her stomach. Her hair had always been long. If there had ever been a point of vanity in Abigail Avery, it would have been her hair. But tonight she was going to get it cut and dyed a different color. She had to admit that part of the nervousness she felt was excitement about the pending change in her appearance.

Just before Desh knocked on the door, it was swung open. As far as Abigail could see in the dim light, Mabelle Henley hadn't changed one bit since their school days. Abigail felt as if she'd been transported back in time.

"Y'all come on in," Mabelle said, stepping aside, then closing the door and locking it as soon as they were inside.

She turned and led them to the salon where dim lighting cast an eerie glow over the equipment.

"I'll have to leave the lights off, or Sheriff Lucas will come nosing around to see why I'm here at this hour. But it's light enough at this station that I can see what I'm doing," she said, finally turning to face them.

As soon as her eyes rested on Abigail, her mouth dropped open.

"Abigail? Abigail Avery?"

"Well, so much for thinking no one would recognize you," Desh said.

"Hi, Mabelle," Abigail said, amazed that the small woman had recognized her so quickly.

"Wow! Abigail, you've changed. You've—you've become a beautiful woman!" Mabelle gushed.

"Thank you, but how did you know it was me? I've been away for a long time, and you're right, I've changed a lot. I didn't think anyone would recognize me."

"It's your hair and eyes," Mabelle answered. "When we were in school, I thought you had beautiful hair, but it was your eyes I loved. When you looked at me I thought you had the softest, kindest blue eyes in the world. And then that day you took up for me when Ned Thompson shoved me down and tried to hold me on the ground, I knew I'd always think of you as a friend."

"How did she take up for you?" Desh asked, intrigued at the thought of his Abigail taking up for anyone, since she always seemed like the victim to him.

"She picked up a big stick and whacked him across the back. He got up and chased after her, but she outran him. But it gave me a chance to get away from him. I told the teacher and got him in trouble. I think he still holds it against me for telling the teacher, and I'm sure he still remembers Abigail whacking him. He's the kind of person that hangs on to, and nourishes, his grudges." A smile spread across her face as she opened her arms to give Abigail a big hug.

"Welcome home, Abigail. Who else knows you're here? I haven't heard anything in the Salon about you."

"Nobody knows except the two of us, Mabelle," Desh said. "And that's the way we want to keep it. That's why we want to get her hair cut and colored. So nobody will recognize her."

"But why?" Mabelle asked.

"I want to find out who killed my father and why I was sent to prison for it," Abigail said. "And I think I can do that better if the guilty parties don't know I'm here snooping around."

"So you really didn't do it? I didn't believe you did. I just couldn't see how anyone as kind as you could have killed someone. A lot of other people in town felt the same way. But I heard a few say that if you killed him, he deserved it because of the way he treated you and your mama."

Abigail was surprised to find that she'd been the topic of discussion in this small town. She'd always felt so invisible and insignificant, she didn't think anyone even knew she existed.

Mabelle started working on Abigail's hair, and the talk turned lighter as Mabelle and Desh discussed local people and happenings. Abigail recognized a few names of the people they talked about, but some were strangers to her.

"*Mrs.* Harry Haney came in today for a manicure," Mabelle said, unexpectedly. "She had two broken nails and the rest were pretty dirty looking. When I asked her if she'd been gardening, she just laughed and said, '*More like getting rid of trash.*' I thought it was kind of weird the way she said it. It's been on my mind all day."

Abigail's eyes flashed to Desh, who gave the slightest shake of his head, as a warning not to say anything.

"Well, maybe she'd been taking stuff to the dump," he volunteered.

"Yeah, I guess. But that woman's strange. I just don't trust her. And I really don't like her. I'd rather she didn't come in my place of business, but I know I can't refuse to wait on her.

"Hmmm. Let's see. What would be a good style for you?" Mabelle asked as she picked up the scissors. "If you're a real estate woman, you'll want a modern, feisty look, right?"

"Whatever you think. As you know, I've been out of circulation, so I'm not sure what the going look for real estate people is," Abigail said.

"I think very short will look good. Since your hair is naturally curly, all you'll have to do is shampoo it, fluff it and go. It'll be totally maintenance free."

"That's pretty much the way it is now," Abigail responded.

Desh growled a slight moan and headed for a far corner of the salon as Mabelle picked up a strand of Abigail's hair and headed toward it with the scissors. He couldn't bear to stand and watch that beautiful hair fall to the floor. He knew it had to be done, but he sure didn't have to watch.

Abigail felt an initial shock as the first clump of hair hit the floor, then determination set in and she watched the transformation take place. She didn't care what it took. She wanted to be able to move around this town freely and proceed with the mission she had come back for.

She could hardly believe all that she'd already found out in the short time she'd been home. What would tomorrow hold? But after seeing her house trashed and hearing Desh talk about the judge's wife, it didn't take long for Desh to convince her she'd be safer staying with him. And his reasoning did make sense. It would arouse less suspicion if she weren't seen around her house.

"Okay, Desh, you can come out of hiding and look at the new beauty queen," Mabelle said.

Abigail had been so lost in her reverie that she'd forgotten to pay attention. Her eyes snapped open at the sound of Mabelle's voice, and she didn't recognize the person looking back at her from the mirror.

Blond streaks and highlights mixed with her natural red formed a halo of beautifully colored curls around her face. In the dim light, her hair had an iridescent glow.

Loud pounding on the front door brought them all to a halt. "Mabelle, is that you in there?" Sheriff Lucas' voice called.

"Oh, crap!" Mabelle whispered. "Desh, you two go! We'll talk tomorrow. I'll head him off and keep him busy while you get out the back door. Hurry!"

"Mabelle!" Again, pounding. His voice grew louder.

"Remember, mum's the word," Desh reminded Mabelle.

"Don't worry, Desh, I've got y'all covered. Now get out of here!"

"Coming! Hold your horses!" They heard Mabelle yell as they escaped out the back door and closed it softly behind them.

In no time Desh and Abigail were around the corner from Mabelle's Salon, and were sure that Sheriff Lucas hadn't seen them leave.

"What will she tell him?" Abigail wondered.

"Knowing Mabelle, she already had a story made up just in case this happened. She can handle Sheriff Lucas."

"Do you think she'll tell anyone about me?"

"Are you kidding? Didn't you see the excitement in her eyes when we were talking about catching the people who did this to you? She'll be our finest asset. Working in a beauty salon, she'll hear all kinds of gossip, and I have the feeling that she'll tell us anything she hears.

"And besides that, I was surprised to see how much she likes you. She has some very good memories of you. That puts her on our side, even more."

"Okay, let me see your new look," Desh said as he turned on the lights in the living room. They'd come straight back to his house after leaving Mabelle's.

Shyness washed over Abigail as she waited for Desh's reaction. It had been a long time since Abigail Avery had felt shy. She didn't like the feeling and couldn't understand why she cared if Desh liked what he saw or not.

He came to her and stopped just before their bodies touched. Her first impulse was to back away, but his hands on her shoulders stopped her.

"You look like one of those baby dolls I used to see in the stores at Christmas time." His voice was barely above a whisper. "The blond highlights really make those big blue eyes stand out. I should have known it wasn't the hair that made you beautiful, Abigail Avery. It's who you are that makes you beautiful." His breath fanned the new, bouncy curls around her face as he spoke.

His hands slowly slid from her shoulders to the base of her neck. Softly his thumbs circled sensitive skin that couldn't hide her pounding pulse. His eyes dropped to the spot just before he lowered his head and replaced his thumbs with his lips. He felt, more than heard, her sharp intake of breath, and raised his lips to her slightly open mouth.

Sweet, just like he'd always imagined. Soft and sweet and yielding. But he had to stop. It wasn't time yet to make his full declaration of love. He didn't want to make her wary of him. So with the greatest of efforts he reluctantly dragged his lips from hers.

"Absolutely beautiful," he whispered, gazing into her half-closed smoky eyes.

Abigail tried to speak, but her voice didn't cooperate. She needed to move away from Desh, but her feet wouldn't obey her commands. So she just stood there and gazed into his brilliant green eyes.

With a groan that was more like a growl, he gathered her close in his arms and held her tightly for a brief moment before releasing her and stepping back.

"It's been a long day, Abigail. Maybe we should call it a night before I do something really stupid." He shoved his hands in his pockets to keep them from reaching for her again.

Sitting on the side of her bed, Abigail waited for her pounding heart to slow down. She didn't think it would ever get back to normal after *that* kiss. Her first real kiss. Twenty-eight years old and just experiencing her first kiss. How bizarre was that! Emotions she should have experienced as a teenager were new to her. Emotions she didn't know existed. Emotions she didn't know how to deal with.

"I don't need this right now," she moaned, and lay back on the bed. She had too many other things to occupy her mind. She had to think about getting revenge on a town.

Yes, that's what she needed to be thinking about, she decided, kicking off her shoes and curling up on the bed. She'd put her gown on later. Right now she had to think about *anything* except Dashing Desh and the way he'd looked at her. Or how gently his hands had caressed the base of her neck. Or how his lips had felt as they claimed hers.

The only light in the room was the angel nightlight, casting its soft glow on the surroundings, and, seemingly, casting a spell on Abigail. As she thought about *nothing* except Desh Elliot, she drifted into sleep with a smile on her face. Abigail Avery had never gone to sleep with a smile on her face.

She didn't know how long she'd been asleep when she heard the distant truck motor. She listened to see if she could tell the direction the sound was coming from. At first it seemed to be filling the room, but as she slid to the side of the bed and listened more closely, it sounded like it was coming from the corner of the room, which made no sense at all. The window was on the opposite side of the room. How could sound be coming from a corner?

Following her ears, she moved toward what she knew was definitely some kind of vehicle. Maybe more than one. And it sounded like gears were changing, like the vehicle was on the move.

In the corner she discovered a vent that she hadn't noticed before. Kneeling down and putting her ear closer to the vent, the sounds became much more distinct. A big vehicle, like a semi or dump truck, was on the move, and it sounded like it was *under* Desh's house! How could that be?

The caves? Something was going on in the caves, and somehow the sound was coming through the vent! But why just this vent? Why didn't Desh hear it? Or did he? Did he know what was going on? When she'd mentioned hearing the trucks this morning, had he told her she was dreaming to throw her off?

As the troubling thoughts swirled in her head, the sound of the vehicle faded into the distance until she couldn't hear it.

Tomorrow she'd find out where this vent led to, she promised herself. She'd also check out other vents in the house to see where they were and why Desh wasn't hearing the same sounds she was. If, indeed, he wasn't hearing them.

She put on the gown she'd worn the night before and went to the bathroom to wash her face. When she caught her reflection in the mirror, she gasped and almost stepped back. She'd forgotten about her new look!

Seeing her short, blond-streaked curls brought the entire day back with a rush. Especially the ending of the day.

She doubted she'd get any more sleep tonight, but she got back into the big, comfortable bed. At least she could lie here and rest.

Thoughts ran rampant in her head, as she knew they would, but finally, from sheer exhaustion, she slept.

Desh Elliot reluctantly opened his eyes at the sound of Major, his pet rooster, crowing his six A.M. wake up call. Desh would never need an alarm clock as long as he had his huge Rhode Island Red. But this morning he'd prefer that Major take his blaring noise somewhere else. Desh hadn't had a very good night.

Having Abigail in the same house was much harder than he'd expected. Much harder. He'd known for a long time that he couldn't allow her to go back to her house when she got out of prison. But things had taken a dangerous turn quicker than he'd expected. Yesterday had proven that.

He'd found a note at the stakeout spot that someone had lost. The scrawled words on the plain piece of paper gave Desh chills every time he remembered them.

Eliminate whoever is snooping around the house.

This was turning into very serious business. He had to speed up his investigation. But he had to work overtime to protect Abigail, because she was set on finding out who had railroaded her to prison. He knew they were all the same. He just wasn't sure why, yet.

Part of his problem for the past couple of days was that he couldn't think of anything except Abigail. She'd invaded his senses. Everything about her intrigued him. He'd obsessed over her when they were in school, but this was worse. He had to find a way to get her out of his head long enough to put his mind to the task of finding out why some Leaky Springs citizens wanted Abigail's property so badly.

He'd spent half the night turning and tossing, his thoughts going from Abigail and how she had yielded to his kiss, to that all-telling note he'd found. And when he did go to sleep, he'd dreamed of fighting a horrible monster because it was trying to abduct Abigail.

Major gave another piercing reminder that Desh needed to get up and get the day started. "Yeah, yeah," he muttered to the rooster. "Keep this up and you'll find yourself part of a pot of chicken dumplings!"

He made his way to the kitchen and started a pot of coffee. He'd wake Abigail up so she could dress while the coffee made. They had a lot to do today.

He knocked quietly on her door. He didn't want to startle her like he'd done yesterday morning. "Abigail? Wake up. I've got coffee brewing."

No response. He knocked a little louder. "Abigail! Are you awake?"

After waiting a few more seconds and not hearing anything, he gently opened the door. Her bed was made, so she was already up. She must be in the bathroom. He stepped inside the room in order to see the bathroom door, but it was open. Walking closer he called, "Abigail, are you in there?" No answer.

Apprehension spiked the hair on the back of his neck. Boldly, he went into the bathroom. Too bad if she was naked. She should answer him.

The bathroom was empty.

Chapter 7

A dim pink tint of sky outside Abigail's window indicated that the sun was rising. She'd done nothing but toss and turn after hearing the truck motor during the night. So getting out of bed, she quickly straightened the room, then dressed.

Quietly easing to the door, she listened to the silent house. Desh was still asleep. Now was a good time to do her search. Common sense told her the vent in her room would lead to a heating and cooling unit. But where on earth could it be? Especially to bring in sounds that seemed to be coming from under the house.

She'd just go outside and walk around the house until she found it. Surely it was light enough for her to find her way around. It would be, soon, and if her luck held, maybe Desh would sleep for a while longer. He'd have more of a chance if that stupid rooster would stop crowing.

Easing down the stairs, hoping one of them didn't creak, she made her way to the front door. She realized she didn't even know where a back door was, other than the one that led to the cellar. The cellar! Was that where the unit was? Maybe that's why the sounds were so clear.

She'd check there first. In the kitchen, she remembered Desh had locked the door that led to the cellar. But she hadn't paid attention to where he put the key. Did he keep it on his key chain? That could pose a problem.

Not daring to turn on a light, Abigail used the dim light that stayed on in the kitchen to try to see if a key was hanging on the wall beside the doorjamb. Nothing. Maybe the key was lying on a shelf.

A sudden gurgling, sputtering sound startled Abigail so badly she felt weak. She'd been so intent on her quest to get into the basement that she hadn't paid any attention to the wonderful scent of morning coffee until the coffee pot signaled its finished cycle.

Drat! Desh must be up. Either that or he had a timer on the coffee pot so it would be ready when he got up. Either way, she didn't have any time to waste. He would be up and in here for that coffee. She was tempted to grab a cup while she searched, but decided against it.

She turned her attention to a small curio cabinet in the corner closest to the cellar door. Maybe the key was there. She pulled on the doors to the cabinet and to her relief they opened. Beautiful little knickknacks tried to shimmer in the dim light. Abigail reminded herself to look at these closer, soon, but not now. Peering into a small gold-trimmed urn, she found what she was looking for.

"Bingo!" she whispered. She took the key and turned directly into Desh's firm chest.

"Can I help you find something, Abigail?" He placed his hands on each of her arms to steady her.

"Uh, no. I was just looking at your pretty things," she said, guiltily clasping her hands behind her back.

Desh slowly slid his hands down her arms, following as

they curved behind her back, to enclose her clasped hands.

"What's in your hands?"

"Nothing," Abigail lied. Emotions boiled inside her at the close proximity of Desh's chest to her own. His breath caressed her ear as he talked. She wanted him to kiss her again. She needed to know if last night's kiss had really been as good as it had seemed.

Not moving anything except his face, Desh gently kissed her ear, her neck, her cheek, then, after what seemed like an eternity, he captured her lips.

Lifting his mouth from hers just enough to speak, he whispered, "It's not nice to lie, Abigail."

She tried to speak, but his lips still rested lightly against hers, barely touching. Stealing the breath from her very lungs. Was the pounding heart hers or his?

"I'm not lying," she finally managed. And again his lips captured hers. Probing. Exploring. Tasting.

"Then what is this?" he asked, prying her hands open and taking the key from the one that held it.

"Oh, that," she said, and tried to turn away from him.

He turned her back to face him. "Abigail, why do you need the key to the cellar? And if you needed it, why didn't you just ask me for it?"

"I heard the truck or trucks again last night. And since you didn't believe me the first time, I thought I'd just explore by myself."

"But why the cellar?"

"Because the sounds were coming from a vent in my bedroom that seemed to be coming from under the house. The only thing that made sense to me was that the vent led to the heating unit, which was probably in the cellar."

"So you think I have trucks in my cellar?"

"No. But I think there may be trucks somewhere in the caves, and the sounds are traveling through the vents. Have you never heard them from the vents in your room?"

"I've just run a few vents, so far. The house didn't have any heating or cooling when I bought it, so this unit is new. My room doesn't have a vent yet. But you're right, the unit is in the cellar." No need to tell Abigail that he'd completed the room she was in first, so it would be ready when she came home. He didn't think it would go over too well if she thought he'd planned for her to stay with him all along.

He went to the coffee pot, poured two cups and set them on the table, then pulled out a chair for Abigail.

"Hmmm. But why would trucks be in the caves?" he pondered aloud. "There are openings in those caves that are large enough for trucks to go through, but why would anyone need to? Where would they be going?"

"That's what I was going to try and find out," Abigail said.

"Abigail, you have to listen to me. You *must not* do any exploring alone. It's just too dangerous. Promise me that you'll only explore when you're with me."

"Desh, I appreciate your concern, but you seem to forget that I've come home to get to the bottom of some things. I can't wait for you to help me. You have your own life to live. A job to take care of. So I can't promise you this. I simply won't sit around and wait for you. I'm beginning to believe the caves have something to do with why these people want my property. So I have to know what's going on."

"Maybe so. But before we jump to any conclusions, let me—us—look around and see if we can find any tracks. Possibly the tracks will lead us to an answer."

"When can we start?"

"What about tonight? If you're hearing the sounds at night, then we might even be able to catch someone in the act. In the meantime, I need to go into town and try to get some work done. Do you want to come with me?"

Standing, Desh slipped the cellar key onto his key chain and put them in his pocket. He winked at Abigail and said, "For your own safety."

She gazed unsmiling into his eyes and thought, *There are more ways into the caves than your cellar door, Dashing Desh.* But aloud, she said, "First it was my old man trying to keep me from the caves, now you."

Desh gathered up their coffee cups and put them in the dishwasher. "Maybe everything your dad did wasn't so bad. Maybe he cared for you more than you realized."

Anger burned through Abigail. What did Desh Elliot know about her relationship with her dad? Neither he nor anyone else had any idea how hard it was to live with her father. She was an emotionally impaired person because of the abuse she'd suffered from him. If he'd cared for her, it had been his best kept secret!

"I'm sorry, Abigail. I shouldn't have said that," Desh said, coming close to her. He'd seen the flash of anger that turned her smoky blue eyes to cold steel. He'd only seen that look in his Abigail's eyes once. That day in court when the judge had pronounced her guilty and sentenced her to prison, he'd watched in awe as she glared coldly at each juror.

Slowly she gained control of the angry lump in the pit of her stomach. It had taken her five of the ten years she'd been in prison to calm that lump to a place where she wasn't constantly aware of it. It only flared up occasionally, now. The way she controlled it was to promise herself that soon—very soon—those people would pay. She could never make her father pay for what he'd done to her, but these others—they would pay.

Taking a deep breath, she moved away from Desh. "It's okay. You grew up in a loving home, so you can't even imagine what it was like for me. But, trust me, my dad didn't care for me at all. Whatever he did was for him. Period."

"But he did provide a home for you. And food. And he

made sure you finished school." Desh knew he was treading on quicksand, but he felt compelled to continue. "There are a lot of kids whose parents don't do that much."

Abigail could only stare at Desh. Whose side was he on, anyway? Now he was taking up for her loser father?

But she had to admit he was right. She'd heard horror stories from the other women in prison. Some had been locked in closets for days when they'd "misbehaved." Some had been starved. Abandoned. Sexually abused. When she thought about it, her situation would have seemed pretty good to some of them.

But that didn't matter. Desh still didn't have the right to preach to her.

Abigail sat in Ma Tucker's Cafe waiting for Desh to meet her for lunch, as he'd requested. He'd insisted on giving her money to buy new clothes, saying that if she was going to pose as a realtor, she needed to look like one.

As she thought about all the garments in the bags surrounding her, the hint of a smile lifted the corners of her mouth. She'd realized soon into her shopping spree that she'd never been shopping for herself. And she'd realized that even though it was hard work, she enjoyed it!

The sales clerks had been very helpful to Abigail. Once she told them what her line of work was, they'd made suggestions of what she might be interested in. She'd tried to keep her look professional, but because of the frumpy way her dad had insisted she dress as a child, and after wearing a prison uniform for ten years, Abigail couldn't help but be drawn to beautiful colors and softer, more feminine styles. She hoped she would look the part she was supposed to be playing.

Suddenly her attention was drawn to two men coming into the small café. They looked vaguely familiar, but she couldn't put a name to them. Did she go to school with them?

Were they on the jury?

Ten years made a big difference in the way some people looked. She'd known that coming back here and finding everyone might prove difficult, but with the right questions asked in the right places, she had no doubt she could find the sleazeballs she was looking for.

Abigail had chosen a table facing the front door so she could see who came in, but her back was actually to the room. As she pondered the identity of the two latest arrivals, she realized the waitress was seating them at the table beside, but slightly behind her, and that she could hear their conversation.

"Have you heard anything?" a high-pitched, whiny voice asked. Of course! Sam Tanner! He owned Tanner's Hardware store. Or he did ten years ago. It would be hard to forget a voice like Sam's.

"No. Not a thing. And we sent the letter last week. We usually get an immediate response. Wonder what the deal is." She didn't recognize the second voice.

Abigail looked up and recognized an older Sheriff Lucas coming through the door. He glanced around the room, then made his way in her direction. Her heart leapt into her throat and stopped. But instead of coming to her table, he pulled out a chair and sat down with the men she'd been listening to.

"She's out!"

"What?" The two said in unison.

"Judge Haney got the notification from the parole board yesterday. She's out on good behavior."

Immobilized, Abigail realized they were talking about her. Her pounding heart almost drowned out their voices. Sweat beaded in her palms.

"We're supposed to watch for her. Look for anyone who fits her description. Judge thinks she'll make a bee-line back here and try to set up housekeeping where she grew up."

"Well, that would be the logical thing, wouldn't it?" Sam's

whiny voice rationalized.

"I don't know, Sam. Would you want to come back and live in a house where your father had been murdered?" Sheriff Lucas condescendingly replied to the other man, then continued, "What do you think, Tom? You think she'll try to live in the old house?"

Tom Culpepper? The state-appointed defense attorney who had haphazardly defended her at her trial? Wow! Ten years had not been kind to him.

"First, you need to watch what you say, Lucas," Tom admonished.

"Huh?"

"She's coming back to a house where *she* murdered her father, not where her father *was* murdered," he ground out his rebuke.

"Oh, yeah, right."

Abigail glanced up to see Desh walking in. He looked around the room until he spotted the table of men behind Abigail. She saw his face tense just the slightest before his eyes found hers. Giving her the briefest signal to follow him, he turned and left the building.

Understanding that he didn't want to sit this close to the threesome and raise any unwanted attention, Abigail stood and gathered her shopping bags, making sure she kept her face averted from the other table. As she walked by them, she heard Sam ask, "Who's that?"

"Don't know," Sheriff Lucas answered. "But I ain't seen her around. She must be new in town."

Abigail quickly paid for her iced tea and left. A shiver ran up her spine as she walked past the window, knowing their attention was still on her. It was going to be hard to separate the interest she got from being a stranger in this small town from her fear of being recognized.

Luckily Desh had parked in a spot that couldn't be seen

from the small café, and was waiting for her in the car.

"What are the odds of that happening?" he asked, as she pushed her bags in the back seat and got in beside him. "I knew the café would have people eating lunch, but I never dreamed about those three being there together. In fact, I've never seen those three together at all."

"Well, it seems they were discussing me."

"What?"

"Judge Haney told them I was out of prison, and to keep an eye out for me. Told them to watch my house to see if I came home to try to live."

"And so it begins," Desh said quietly.

"And get this, Desh. Sheriff Lucas asked if they thought I'd really come back to the house where my dad had been murdered!"

"He used that word?"

"Yes. Then Tom really got on him and told him to watch what he said."

"Too bad you didn't have a tape recorder," Desh muttered as he pulled away from the curb.

"They were talking about me when I left."

"About where you might be?"

"No. About *me*. Being a new person in town. Wondering who I was."

"Well, that's natural. People are going to do that in a small town where everyone knows everybody and everybody's business."

"I know. But it still makes me nervous. I'm never sure when someone will recognize me."

"Abigail, I don't think your own father would recognize you now. Especially with the new hair."

"And wait until you see the clothes I bought today. The Abigail Avery that this town knew never dreamed about wearing clothes like this!"

At Desh's moan, Abigail glanced at him. His head rested against the back of the seat and one hand was clasped over his heart as he said, "I don't know if my heart can take a fancy-dressed Abigail Avery, with her hair all short and sexy."

Abigail did something she hadn't done many times in her life. She laughed out loud. And it felt very good.

Chapter 8

"**This looks like a good spot,**" **Desh said.** The wall of the cave was dry and the ground was smooth. It would be fairly comfortable for them to sit and wait for the truck sounds Abigail had heard.

Desh held the large flashlight high and checked the surrounding wall and ground. "Make sure no critters are camping with us," he said, giving Abigail an impious wink. "After you, ma'am," he said, offering Abigail a hand as she sat down and leaned back against the cool wall. When he took his place beside her, the length of his thigh pressed against hers. "I think it will be safer if I turn this flashlight off. We don't want to alert anyone that we're here."

With that, darkness like Abigail didn't know could exist surrounded them. Absolute, tangible darkness.

Desh felt the shudder that ran through her body, and reached over and took her hand in his.

"So what time do you think it was when you heard the vehicles?" His voice penetrated the darkness, giving Abigail an anchor to settle her churning nerves.

"I'm not sure when I'd initially heard them, but the first night they woke me up at least three times. Last night, I only heard them once. It was between midnight and dawn, the first night. Last night it was around midnight."

"Well, we may have a couple of hours to wait. Maybe even longer. Or it's a possibility that the sounds aren't coming from down here, so we may not hear anything," Desh said.

And maybe you don't believe I heard anything, Abigail thought.

"We probably should have waited in your room," Desh added. "That would have been a lot more comfortable. And I can think of a much better way to pass the time in your room." His voice became a soft caress as he placed an arm around Abigail's shoulder.

Abigail's surprised intake of breath gave Desh access to her slightly parted lips as his cool mouth covered hers.

"You're like a drug for me, Abigail. Once I had a taste of you, I can't think of anything else."

"Desh—"

"It's okay. I'm not going to force myself on you in this dark cave. When we make love I want to be able to see you. I want to watch your face." He pulled her head down to rest on his shoulder. "Try to get a nap if you want to. This may be a long wait."

A nap? Sleep was the last thing on Abigail's mind as she rested her head on Desh's shoulder. Had he actually said 'when we make love'? *When we make love?*

It seemed that Dashing Desh Elliot had plans of his own that Abigail couldn't get a grasp on. The fact that he'd even want to make love to her was too hard for her to grasp. Why would Dashing Desh Elliot want to make love to Abigail Avery? Especially now that he seemed to be a successful businessman, and she was an ex-convict? They were even farther apart on the social scale now than they were in school.

This was just too much to think about. All she'd wanted to do was come back here and find out who had killed her father and blamed it on her. She didn't need her mind cluttered with trying to figure out what Desh's part in all this was. Or why he even had a part in it. And she sure didn't have time to fight with the confused emotions that flooded her when he was around.

As her troubled thoughts swirled through her mind, Abigail relaxed and was soon asleep.

Desh smiled as her breathing became deep and rhythmic. She hadn't commented on his statement about making love to her. He planned to drop these little innuendos on her occasionally so she would get used to hearing how he felt about her.

He rested his face against her hair and breathed in the sweet smell of his Abigail. Desh Elliot was a patient man. He'd waited ten years for moments like this. He could wait as long as it took for Abigail to love him as much as he loved her.

They came awake at the same time. A roaring noise surrounded them, as if they were about to be run over by a steamroller. But there were no lights, no smell of exhaust—nothing that would indicate that a vehicle was close to them.

Desh pulled Abigail to her feet. He switched on the flashlight and gave a quick perusal of their surroundings to confirm that they weren't about to be run down. Only the eerie cave walls surrounded them, so he turned the light off.

As the noise abated slightly, Desh leaned close to Abigail's ear and said, "There must be another level to this cave system, because there is no way or no where a vehicle that big could have passed us."

Just as Abigail was about to answer him, they were once again engulfed by another approaching truck. Or, at least it sounded like a truck. A very big truck.

As it followed the first one and eventually faded into the distance, quiet settled back around the two waiting people.

"Let's go back to the house," Desh suggested. "We can check this out later. I don't think it would be safe for us to traipse around anymore tonight."

Abigail was only too happy to agree with him, and they made their way back to Desh's house. She felt cold and stiff from being in the cave. How long had they been there? She couldn't believe she'd actually fallen asleep with her head on Desh's shoulder! Had he slept?

"I'm sorry I doubted you, Abigail," Desh said, closing and locking the door to the cellar.

The warmth and familiar lights of his kitchen sent a calming through her.

"Well, I'm just relieved that we found the source of my mysterious truck sounds," Abigail answered. "At least I know I'm not imagining things."

"This is getting fascinating," Desh said. His green eyes gleamed with excitement. "I never dreamed that this cave system might have layers to it."

"Maybe they're dumping some kind of illegal hazardous material down there," Abigail suggested.

Desh's jaw dropped as he gazed at Abigail. "Now *that* makes a whole lot of sense. That's just like something the lowlifes who run this town would do."

"But what?" she asked.

"Maybe a whole lot of used tires," he answered. "Let's get some rest and tomorrow we'll go spelunking."

The distant crowing of a rooster brought Abigail out of a deep sleep. She immediately remembered that she and Desh were going to check out the cave this morning, so she bounded eagerly from bed. She dressed hurriedly and headed for the kitchen to see if Desh had made his wonderful coffee yet. Sniffing the air as she went, she picked up on the aroma before she reached the kitchen.

"Ah, the most beautiful spelunker in the world!" Desh said, looking up from the morning paper he'd been reading. He sat at the table with the paper scattered around him. "Sit down and I'll get you some coffee."

"Desh, I can get my own coffee," Abigail protested.

"M'lady, I am at your service," he insisted. "Be seated, and I'll bring your wakeup potion." He pulled out a chair for her.

Awkwardly, Abigail sat down. Having a man fuss over her surely wasn't something she was used to, and she wasn't sure she could ever get used to it.

"After we have a cup of coffee and finish the paper, I'll make some eggs and toast. We need our strength if we're going to have a hard day in the caves."

"What do you expect us to find?"

"I don't have any idea. As I said last night, I didn't dream there was any more to this part of the cave than what I've seen. But those trucks seemed to be *above* us. I know we have to go down slightly when we enter from your place, and there does seem to be an incline as we approach my place, but I still wouldn't think there's enough room up there to drive a truck."

"Maybe the truck wasn't underground. Maybe it was crossing our property and it just sounded like it was in the cave."

"Hmmm. No, those motors were too loud to be outside the cave. I'm not sure where or how, but they were underground. And that's what we're going to try to find out today."

After a hearty breakfast, the two headed underground. They'd walked until Abigail thought they were almost back to her place when Desh took a sudden turn and she thought he was about to walk into the cave wall. But just before they got to the wall, Abigail could see a slight division in the formation of the barrier.

"Now this is what your dad didn't want you to find, Abigail," he said.

He led her into a corridor that was barely wide enough for them to walk through single file. The big flashlight he carried illuminated walls that were as smooth as marble. They appeared man-made and surreal in this underground world.

Without warning the corridor opened into a large room. A small, crystal clear pool glistened as if it had its own light. Abigail realized Desh had turned the flashlight off and a ray of sunlight was actually filtering in from somewhere and shining directly on the pool of water. The room was light enough to look around without the help of the flashlight.

In the far corner she saw what appeared to be some kind of equipment. A table, some pots, and a contraption that didn't make any sense to her. They looked as if they were waiting for someone to return today and use them.

"Your father's small business," Desh explained.

"So, this is where he was when he 'went to work'?"

"As far as I can gather from the townspeople, this is the only job your dad ever had. He furnished a lot of folks with their weekend good-times."

Abigail approached the cluttered array of strange looking objects. As she drew near them, she subconsciously realized a growing dread. Almost fear. She expected her father to start yelling at her about something.

"As odd as it seems," Desh's voice startled her, "the faint scent of old moonshine whiskey still lingers on this paraphernalia."

"That's it!"

"That's what?"

"I had this weird feeling that my dad was around, but it's the smell. This is the way he always smelled when I was a child. One time I asked him why he smelled like he did and he slapped me and told me not to ask people personal questions like that."

"Do you have any *good* memories of your dad?" Desh asked.

"I remember one time when I was really sick with the flu, he actually made some soup and brought it to me. He told me to hurry up and get better because he didn't want to lose me, too. Just for the briefest moment I had the feeling that he was going to tell me he loved me, but he didn't. But, for that brief moment, I kind of felt like he did."

Without warning, Desh pulled her into his arms and held her close. "One day, Abigail, you're going to know how it feels to be loved completely."

Unknown sensations washed through Abigail as Desh's strong arms held her close. Comfort. Peace. Belonging. Strange feelings, yet wonderfully right.

"But right now, we have to find where and how some kind of heavy equipment could pass through this cave," he said, reluctantly releasing her. "It's obviously not here. If another room of the cave was above us, the sun wouldn't be filtering in and shining on that pool. That's open ground up there."

"Maybe they were up there and it just sounded close."

"No, those motors were inside the cave. They echoed too loudly to be outside. We'll just keep looking."

Desh led the way back through the narrow corridor leading to her father's moonshine still. Finding out about this place somehow gave Abigail a little more insight into her father.

Back in the main opening, Desh held the light where he could inspect all the surrounding walls as he headed slowly back the way they'd come.

"Why are we going back?" Abigail asked.

"We were almost to your property, so I'm pretty sure there aren't any openings in that direction. We're looking for any hidden openings like the one we were just in. Any kind of crack or crevice that might open up into a larger room."

"How did you find the still?"

"Purely by accident. When I first discovered the cave connecting our properties, I was pretty excited and spent some time down here just looking around. One day I decided to turn my flashlight off just to see how dark it would be, and I saw a tiny ray of light. I left the flashlight off and felt my way to where the light was flickering on the wall. Once I got close enough to put my hand in the light, I turned the flashlight back on and discovered the corridor. I followed it and discovered what we just saw. Somehow the sun was shining at an angle on the water and it was casting a reflection down the corridor. That's probably how your dad found the spot."

He talked as he walked, shining the light here and there, looking for any crack or crevice in the walls of the cave that he hadn't noticed before.

They carefully searched the walls, floor, ceiling, for over an hour, until they finally made their way back to the entrance of Desh's basement.

"This is turning out to be one big mystery," Desh said. "Nothing!"

"But the vehicles had to be somewhere," Abigail offered.

"Well, apparently, we've overlooked something, or there's just not an opening to the other level of the cave from this passage."

"But how could those motors sound so loud and close if there were solid rock between us and them?"

"That's a very good question, Abigail. One that I don't have an answer for. There's a logical reason, but I can't put my finger on it. But right now, I think we need to get a bite of lunch."

Once back in the kitchen, Desh locked the door to the basement and slipped the keys into his pants pocket, giving

Abigail a wicked wink. "I can't take the risk of you trying to sneak over to your place, so I'm going to hang on to this key."

"There are more ways to my place than this cave, Desh," Abigail stated.

"Now, we've talked about that, Abigail. You *must not* go there where anyone can see you!" The seriousness in Desh's voice brought back the shooting and the tumbled rooms in her house.

"Desh, I came home to find out about my father's murder. I can't find out anything by hiding out at your house or in a cave chasing invisible trucks!"

"I know. I know you're getting frustrated, but I'm convinced that this cave system and those trucks all tie in with your dad's murder. You can't solve this mystery in a week. We're going to have to take this slow and easy or we'll start making people suspicious."

"How slow? I need some answers. I need to be able to go home. I can't just live here with you for an extended length of time."

"Why not? It seems to be working okay. I'm fine with it. In fact, I love having you here. This big old house can feel mighty empty sometimes. Just knowing you're here makes it seem happy and full of life."

"Well, you knew it was a big house when you bought it. Maybe you should get married and fill it up with kids if it's too empty for you."

"That's exactly what I plan to do, Abigail. I've just been waiting for the right woman to come back home."

"Where did she go? Desh, are you in love with someone? Did she leave you? If so, how is she going to feel if she comes home and finds another woman living with you?"

The ringing of the phone interrupted Abigail's barrage of questions.

"Let me get this," Desh said, holding up a hand to signal

her to wait, as he went to the living room to take the call.

Confused thoughts swirled through Abigail's head. If Desh was in love with another woman, why had he said all those things to her? Why had he kissed her?

And why did she care? Why did just thinking about Dashing Desh Elliot loving another woman cause a lump in the pit of her stomach?

"That was Mabelle. She wants us to have dinner with her tonight. She says she may have some information that will help us," Desh said, coming back to the kitchen.

Chapter 9

"Did she hint at what it could be?" Abigail asked.

"No. She said she didn't want to talk about it on the phone. She sounded very mysterious."

"What time?"

"Seven o'clock at Charlie's."

"Do you think there'll be anyone there who might recognize me?"

"Charlie's main busy time is lunch. But like I told you, Abigail, nobody will recognize you now. Just relax and stop worrying."

The rest of the day passed fairly quickly. Desh gave her a tour of the huge old house, and told her of the renovations he wanted to make. She liked his ideas and could envision the house in its finished state. Basically, he planned to restore it to its former grandeur. Apparently it had been in Molly Draper's family since the late 1800s and had been an extravagant house for the time period. It made Abigail wish she knew more about her family history.

"This will be a beautiful home, Desh," Abigail said as the tour ended in the living room. Glancing around, she again experienced shadowy memories. She felt a brief moment of sadness that some other woman would give Desh children and they'd be happy in a house that should be hers. She felt sure that under different circumstances she'd have inherited this house, since she was the only grandchild of the Drapers. Or was she?

"Desh, was my mom an only child?" She held her breath for his answer. Maybe she did have family somewhere.

"Yes, she was an only child. I checked the records before buying the house. I didn't want to run into some kind of belated estate squabble. But I guess we'd better get dressed. We need to leave in about an hour."

Abigail dressed in one of her new outfits and was very pleased with the look. A baby blue blouse tucked into a pair of navy pants with a lightweight white jacket gave her a professional, yet feminine look. At the encouragement of the salesladies, she'd even bought jewelry to match each outfit. So she finished off her ensemble with a silver necklace and earring set.

She felt a little nervous going downstairs to meet Desh. He'd never seen her in anything except the drab gray slacks and blue top she'd brought from prison with her.

He was watching the local weather report when she entered the room, and didn't see her at first. Her heart did a funny flutter when she took in his still-damp blond hair and freshly shaven face. He really *was* dashing in his jeans and white western-cut, long-sleeved shirt, the sleeves rolled up a few turns to expose thick, dark blond hair on his forearms.

He turned and looked into her eyes as if he sensed she was watching him. Flustered, she glanced quickly away.

"Oh, wow!" He turned the TV off and stood up. "*Oh, wow!*" he repeated, and came toward her. "Abigail! You are beautiful! I always thought you were beautiful, but you're radiant in those colors!"

"Thank you," Abigail whispered. She'd never had this kind of compliment bestowed upon her. The closest thing to happiness she'd ever known welled up inside her. For the first time in her life, she felt a hint of confidence. A flash of self-acceptance—of liking herself—eased into her soul.

Mabelle was waiting for them when they got to Charlie's.

A hostess seated them in a far corner of the room, where they wouldn't be so conspicuous to the other diners.

They made small talk until the waiter took their order. But finally Desh turned to Mabelle and asked, "So what did you hear?"

"This may not be anything, but it sounded kind of suspicious to me," she said in a voice so low that Desh and Abigail had to lean toward her to hear. "I was in Kirkland's Feed and Seed early this morning. You know I'm small, so I'm not that easy to see when I'm standing behind a shelf. I was looking for some birdseed when I heard two men talking. It didn't take me long to recognize Judge Haney's voice. I didn't recognize the other voice, though, so I found a way to peek through the shelves, and this guy is new. I've never seen him in Leaky Springs. He's a weird-looking little guy. I'll bet he's no bigger than me. Kind of slimy looking."

She paused while the waiter set their drinks down.

"Anyway, Judge Haney said, 'She's out of prison, and I know she'll come back here. Someone's already been snooping around the house, and I'll bet it's her. We've got to find that package! It hasn't just disappeared off the face of the earth. Dammit! Find the package!' Then the other guy says to Judge Haney, 'Judge, we've looked everywhere I know to look. We've looked in every closet, every drawer, every nook and cranny of that house. I just don't believe it's in the house.' Then Judge

Haney told him to tell the boys to keep looking and if they couldn't find it, and *she* didn't show up soon, they'd just burn the damn house! Then they left the store."

At Abigail's sharply indrawn breath Desh reached out and covered her hand with his. "Trust me, Abigail, they're not going to burn the house until they've found what they're looking for. Apparently they still think it's somewhere in the house, so they won't burn it."

Abigail caught the sharp look Mabelle gave her when Desh placed his hand on hers. Was Mabelle jealous of Desh? Did she have feelings for him? Were they an item and Desh just hadn't mentioned it? Was Mabelle the woman Desh was in love with? He sure didn't act like it, if she was.

The arrival of their meal interrupted Abigail's thoughts and any conversation. But after the waiter left Desh asked Mabelle, "So you've never seen this new guy in town before?"

"No. And trust me, I'd remember him. He's really odd looking. He was totally bald. From where I was it didn't look like he'd ever had a hair on his head! But the main thing was his size. If I hadn't heard his voice, I'd have thought it was a woman with some kind of disease that had caused her to lose all her hair."

"Anything else that would stand out about him if we saw him?"

"His eyes were such a bright blue they looked like they had lights on behind them. Strange looking eyes. I'm telling you, this little dude gives me the creeps just thinking about him!" An involuntary shiver passed over Mabelle.

"Did Judge Haney call him by a name?"

"I didn't hear one, if he did."

"Okay. Mabelle, you've done a magnificent job! You were at the right place at the right time. I really appreciate your help in this. I can't tell you that enough!" Desh placed his hand on hers and squeezed it tightly.

Abigail watched the light spread over Mabelle's face and knew in that instant the woman was in love with Desh. Whether or not he shared the feeling Abigail didn't know, but Mabelle Henley had it bad for Dashing Desh.

"Ladies, I need to go to the boy's room, if you'll excuse me for a few minutes," Desh said, standing up and leaving the table.

For a moment the silence was awkward, but not for long.

"What happened to you?" Mabelle asked, surprising Abigail.

"What do you mean?"

"You used to be so nice and slim, but you got fat in prison."

Abigail was stunned. Nice little Mabelle suddenly didn't seem so nice. What about all the compliments she'd given Abigail the night she cut her hair?

"I guess I got full in prison, Mabelle. I was slim when I was a kid because I didn't always get enough food."

"Really? You mean you really had to go hungry, Abigail?"

"Sometimes. There wasn't always a lot of food around our house. I'm not saying this to make you feel sorry for me. That was just the way it was. But one of the reasons I stayed by myself at school so much at lunch break was because most of the time I didn't have any lunch, and I didn't want anyone to know it."

"Aw, Abigail! I'm so sorry." At least the old Mabelle was back, Abigail thought. But just for a moment.

"Anyway," Mabelle continued, "You're fat now. Are you going to go on a diet and lose some weight?"

"Why on earth would I make myself hungry on purpose?" Abigail couldn't even imagine the concept.

"Because being fat isn't healthy, Abigail. Plus, people just look better when they're slim."

"Well, I'm not planning on entering any beauty contests, Mabelle, so I'm not worried about looking all that good. Besides, I like the way I look now a lot better than the way I used to look. And as far as health's concerned, I know for a fact that I'm a lot healthier now than I used to be."

"Okay. But don't say I didn't try to tell you. At least I won't have to worry about Desh."

"What's that supposed to mean?" Abigail asked.

"Men don't like fat women, so I don't have to worry about Desh being attracted to you."

Abigail remembered Desh's kisses. And all the things he'd said to her since she'd been home. How he'd called her 'his Abigail.'

"Are you sure about that, Mabelle?" she asked. "I'm sure there are some men who like their women to have a little flesh on their bones." She couldn't help the devilish feeling that made her want to get back at Mabelle.

"Maybe so, but I don't think Desh is one of them. Just look at him. He's so handsome. So perfect. He needs a perfect woman to walk beside him through life."

"And you're that perfect woman?"

"Maybe. But I don't know if he knows it yet," Mabelle admitted. "But just so you know, Abigail, I have my eyes set on him, so you just keep your dealings with him on a business level. Otherwise, you're going to get your heart broken. I like you and don't want to hurt you, but I mean to have Desh Elliot. Is that clear?"

"Very," Abigail said. She was seeing a side of Mabelle Henley that she doubted Desh had ever seen.

"Sorry to keep you ladies waiting, but I can see you carried on the conversation without me," Desh said, sitting back down. "I'm glad to see that. I hope you two can be really good friends."

That's probably not going to happen, Abigail thought.

"Oh, I think Abigail and I will get along marvelously," Mabelle put in. "I think we have a real good understanding of each other."

"Desh Elliot! I thought that was you, man!" A booming voice interrupted them. A huge man had walked up and was thumping Desh on the back.

"And who is this beauty you have here?" he asked, indicating Abigail. "I haven't seen her around these parts."

"Hello, Josh," Desh greeted the newcomer. "This is Mary Draper. She's in town checking on property for a client. She's a Realtor."

Abigail admired Desh's quick reaction. They'd forgotten to agree on a name for her, so he'd pulled one out of the hat on the spur of the moment. Ironically, he'd called her by her first name and her mother's maiden name. Had that been on purpose?

"Well, you can't hog her to yourself, boy!" Talking about her as if she wasn't in the room.

"Mary, this is Josh Duncan. We played football together in high school. Ever since then, he's been trying to move in on all my plays! He thinks just because he's the head coach at Leaky Springs High, he's the top dog in these parts."

Abigail extended her hand to have it swallowed up in Josh's huge grasp. Josh dropped to one knee while still holding her hand and said, "Right now, before he has a chance to, I want to propose to you! Will you be my wife?"

"You mean your second wife, you big lug!" A tall, slim woman walked up and whacked Josh across the shoulders with her purse. "Get up off your knees and act like a man!"

Desh, Josh and the woman all broke into laughter before the woman turned to Abigail. "I'm sorry, honey, he makes a fool of himself when he's had too much to drink. I knew when he had that second glass of iced tea, he'd be hard to handle!"

Standing, Josh slipped his arm around the woman.

"Mary, this is Jenny. We've been married for so long I forget sometimes." But as he kissed Jenny's cheek, Abigail could tell they shared a deep love. Josh was just a big joker and Jenny understood him.

As they said their goodbyes, Abigail noticed the cloudy look on Mabelle's face. She realized that Josh and Jenny hadn't even spoken to Mabelle.

"Now there goes a couple of goody-two-shoes," Mabelle ground out.

"Now, Mabelle. Are you still holding a grudge because she got homecoming queen in high school and ran off with the man you wanted to marry?" Desh teased.

"She got homecoming queen, but she didn't get the man I want to marry, Desh. That man is still around and available," Mabelle said. "But they just think they're better than everyone else. I hate it when people put on airs like they do."

Somehow, Abigail felt, there was more to the story than she was hearing, but she was too busy with her own thoughts to worry about Mabelle's problems.

"Desh, are you telling me that's Josh Duncan from school? I'd never have recognized him! He's changed so much! He used to be slim and shy. Now look at him!"

"Yeah, he got fat and loud-mouthed," Mabelle interjected.

"That's what I've been telling you about yourself, Abigail. Just like you didn't recognize Josh, nobody is going to recognize you," Desh reassured her.

"Yeah, because you got fat, too," Mabelle said, forgetting to be nice in front of Desh.

"What?" Desh's voice had suddenly lost its warmth. "What did you say, Mabelle?"

"It's okay, Desh," Abigail said, surprised at the anger in his eyes. "Mabelle was just commenting that I used to be nice and slim, but got fat in prison. There's nothing wrong with that observation. It's what happened."

"Yeah, Desh. I didn't mean anything bad by what I said," Mabelle crawfished.

"So my new name is Mary Draper?" Abigail asked, trying to change the subject.

"I'm sorry to just pull that out of the air, but I realized when Josh walked up that we hadn't come up with a name for you. I hope you don't mind that I chose your first name and Molly's last name," Desh explained.

"No, not at all. I'm just surprised you knew my first name," Abigail said.

"So, Mabelle, if anyone asks you about Abigail, she's Mary Draper, a Realtor in town looking for property for an out-of-town client. That's all you know about her, okay?" "Sounds good to me," Mabelle agreed.

Soon they said their goodnights and left the restaurant.

"Very interesting news that Mabelle had, huh," Desh commented, once they were on their way home.

"Desh, I'm worried about my house. If they burn it down, I won't have anywhere to live," Abigail said.

"They're not going to burn your house down until they find what they're looking for, Abigail. It wouldn't make any sense to destroy the house if they haven't found what they're after."

"What if they've already found the deed? What if they're just waiting for me to show up to try to live there? If they don't want me back in town, it would make sense for them to burn my house so I couldn't live there."

"Well, they know that even if they burn your house, you can always find somewhere to live. Like with me."

"But I can't live with you forever, Desh."

"Why not?"

"Because you'll want to get married someday and have a family. You said so, yourself. I believe it would be a little awkward if I was living with you when that happened."

"Not if you're the woman I marry. But that's another conversation we haven't had yet. Now, I want you to stop worrying about the deed. I don't think Judge Haney and his goons are looking for a deed. Mabelle said they kept mentioning a 'package.' But I also know they haven't found the deed yet, so I believe your house is safe for the time being."

"What makes you so sure they don't have the deed?"

"Because I have it."

Chapter 10

"**What?** *You* have it? How on earth did you wind up with it?"

"It seems, and I'm just guessing here, that when your mom insisted on marrying your dad, your grandparents gave them forty acres to live on. But apparently they never made a will or sold the land to your parents. I'm not sure why. Nor am I sure of all the stipulations, but when I was going over my deed, after I bought the Draper place, I realized it contained the land and your house.

"It's really strange, because when I looked up your place in the tax records, it shows the house and forty acres as if it stands alone. But when I looked at the Draper land plat, it plainly shows your acreage and house.

"I want to look into it more, but not until we find out why some of the townspeople want your place. I'm not sure why they haven't figured out that it's part of the Draper property— my property—but I don't want to raise any questions about it at this point."

"So you're telling me that you own my home and property?

That it's not even mine?" Disbelief flooded Abigail.

"It will always be yours, Abigail. But at this point, it seems that it's in my name."

"Then you're telling me my dad was killed and I spent ten years in prison because of land and a house we didn't even own?"

"That appears to be the case," Desh answered.

"But who paid the taxes on the place?"

"Apparently the Drapers kept the taxes paid until Molly died. When I bought the Draper place, I had to pay some back taxes. And I'm pretty convinced the Drapers had something to do with the fact that your land and house were listed separately from theirs, even though they still owned them. Why else would they have kept the taxes up? Somehow I don't think they wanted it to look like they were connected to your father in any way."

"But surely my dad knew he wasn't paying taxes. And surely he knew who was."

"It was probably an arrangement that was made while your mom was still alive, and he was very aware of who was keeping the taxes up. That's just my guess."

"So after you bought it, you turned the electricity on?"

"Actually, about a year ago, I climbed the light pole and turned it on myself. I knew you'd be coming home soon and I wanted the electricity to be on when you got home. I guess it's that 'light in the window' romantic notion or something.

"Desh! You're stealing electricity?"

"Nope. Just borrowing it. I'll get them to read the meter when this is over, and pay up in full."

"So my grandparents not only didn't care enough about me to try to see me, they didn't care enough about me to make sure I had an inheritance," Abigail said.

"Abigail, they probably knew if they deeded the place to your dad, he'd sell it, and no telling where you would have wound up. I'm sure they did what they did for your mom's and your best interest. At least, they thought they did. Even after your mom died, they knew you had a place to live. So in their own way, they were taking care of you."

"I guess. But why didn't they have a will? I can't believe they both died and didn't leave any kind of will for their house and all this land. How much did they own, anyway?"

"Two hundred acres."

"And you bought it all?"

"Yes."

"Still. Why didn't they leave something to me if they cared anything at all about me?"

"I don't know. I know that Jim had a stroke before you ever went to prison, and was in a nursing home until he died. Maybe Molly just forgot they didn't have a will. She was getting pretty old by then. She died about a year after you went to prison."

"I just can't believe this," Abigail said. She had nothing! She was a twenty-eight year old ex-convict with nothing! No family, no home, no money. Nothing.

"Abigail? Are you okay?" Desh reached out and placed his arm on the back of the car seat.

Abigail realized they were back at his place, and he'd parked the car.

"No, Desh, I'm not okay, right now," she said, opening her door and getting out of the car. "I have to be alone and try to think some of this through." She rushed to her room as soon as Desh let them in the house.

Desh stood and watched her hurry from him. He wished she trusted him enough to allow him to comfort her. But he understood that she'd spent all her life alone, and any comfort she got came from her own ability to work through a situation. He yearned to hold her and make her burdens disappear.

"Soon, my love," he whispered. "Soon you'll have more

than you ever dreamed of. If you'll just allow it to happen."

Across town, Josh Duncan picked up his phone and dialed a number. "Who is Mary Draper, and why is she in town checking into property for an out-of-town client? What property is she checking on and who is the client?"

"What are you talking about?" The voice on the other end of the line sounded slightly irritated that he'd been disturbed.

"I'm talking about a woman I met tonight. She was having dinner with Desh Elliot and Mabelle Henley. She's a very attractive, large woman with strange-colored blue eyes and short reddish-blond hair. In fact, her eyes keep reminding me of someone. I know I've seen eyes like that somewhere, but I can't remember where. It seems like a long time ago." He paused for a moment as if trying to force the memory to come back.

"Did you call me to talk about some woman's eyes?" The voice on the other end was becoming truly annoyed now.

"No, Uncle Harry. I called to tell you that those goons you hired as private detectives aren't doing their job. They should be aware of any and every new person who comes into this town. Whether it's Abigail Avery or not! Now I'm putting my reputation, my job, and probably my marriage on the line by letting you use the equipment that was in my dad's shop, so I don't want anything to go wrong. I don't want anyone to know that I'm involved with you, at all! Do you understand me, Uncle Harry?"

"Don't get your pants in a wad, boy! I'm your uncle. I'm going to take care of you. I took care of your dad, didn't I?"

"I still haven't decided if you did or not," Josh answered. "Just find out who she is, okay?"

"Alright, already! Look, I saw this woman the other day. I told her there was no property in this area for sale and for her to just move on. I'm sure she will be gone in a day or two."

"Well, I sure hope so. Strangers in Leaky Springs make us all nervous."

"Well, go take a nerve pill, I'm busy!"

Judge Harry Haney slammed the phone down and went back to his first love. His computer. The Internet—what a wonderful invention! His smile became vulgar and his pulse-rate quickened as he continued to search the sites he loved so much.

In her room Abigail sat on her bed and opened a worn, brown manila folder. She took out a piece of paper and read over the names. The writing was ten years old and becoming faded from the many times she'd held the paper and read the names. One by one, she went over each name and again saw the face of each one as the person looked back at her from the jurors' section.

Judge Harry Haney. The first name on the list, and faded worse from the times Abigail had run her thumb over the name as she made her promise of retribution.

Ned and Jeb Thompson, and their father, Roy. Roy was dead, so she guessed she should mark his name off the list, but not yet. No name came off the list, yet.

Sam Tanner. Sam had always seemed to befriend her father, so it was hard to understand why he had been involved. But she was sure everyone on the jury was put there for one purpose. To send her to prison. To get her out of the way.

Jim Duncan. Josh's father, who owned a garage that did maintenance on big trucks and equipment.

Dan Tucker. Dan owned the largest furniture store in the area. People traveled for miles to come and buy their furniture from him.

These were all businessmen. They or their ancestors had been businessmen in Leaky Springs for years on end. So why they would want her father dead? And why would they want to send Abigail to prison for her property?

But the other six who had served on the jury were even more of a puzzle. *Ella Mae Jones, Becky Brewer, Jane Haley, Connie Ivy, Louise Long,* and *Ferbie Singly* were all widows or divorcees with children. These women's involvement made less sense than the businessmen.

If the businessmen in the community were all working together to get her property, as Desh speculated, she could understand that they'd frame her. But she couldn't come up with one single reason why these women would be involved.

A soft knock on the door startled Abigail out of her deep concentration.

"Yes?" she called.

"Are you okay?" Desh asked, opening the door to peer in.

"Yes, I'm fine," she answered, forgetting to hide the list from him.

"Do you want to talk about it?" he asked.

"About what?" Abigail had been in such deep thought over her list that she'd temporarily forgotten about their earlier conversation.

"About me owning your property," Desh reminded her. Puzzled that she would even ask what, he moved closer to see what she held in her hand.

"No. I haven't had time to think about that yet," she answered, unconsciously rubbing her thumb over the list as she'd done so many times in the past. As if just touching the list of names would conjure up some answers.

"What's that?" Desh asked.

"What? Oh, this." Abigail promptly pushed the list back inside the envelope to hide it.

"Abigail, if I'm going to help you, you don't need to hide things from me."

"Oh, alright. But this won't help us. It's just something

that's kept me going for the past ten years," she said, handing him the worn list. "This is a list of—"

"The jurors who sent you to prison," Desh finished for her, recognizing the list of names.

"Yes. But how did you know that?"

"I have the same list, Abigail. And I've probably gone over my list as many times as you have yours."

Surprised, again, at how deeply he seemed to be involved in her case, Abigail said, "I've tried so hard to figure out how the men could be connected, and why they'd do it, but the women make even less sense. From what little I knew about those women, they were all widows or divorcees, and very poor. What could they possibly want from my father or me? Did they hate my dad for some reason and just want to get back at me? Why?" Frustration edged her voice.

"I have a theory that they all needed money badly enough to take a bribe."

"You think they were paid to find me guilty?" Disbelief flooded Abigail. Yet, this made more sense than anything she'd come up with.

"Yes. Since I couldn't think of a reason for these women to be on the jury, they were the first ones I did research on. At the time you went to jail, they were all living in poverty conditions. Then, suddenly, they all wound up with new items. Becky, Jane and Connie, the three divorcees with children, all had new houses within the year. Ella Mae unexpectedly moved up North to live with a sister, and Louise and Ferbie were able to move to a new retirement center. They're both dead now, and I would probably have a hard time finding Ella Mae, but I think we should talk with Becky and Jane. Connie got remarried a few years ago and moved away, so it might be hard to locate her."

"Great! Let's talk with Becky and Jane tomorrow!"

"Well, we can't do it tomorrow. That's one of the reasons

I came up here. I wanted to check on you, but I forgot to tell you that I have to take Dad to Birmingham tomorrow for his yearly heart checkup. We'll be gone a couple of days."

"Did your dad have a heart attack recently?"

"He had open heart surgery two years ago. He had it done in Birmingham, since that's the closest heart specialist to us. So I have to take him back on a yearly basis to have his checkups. He did extremely well, and continues to do well, but they still have to check him."

"So you'll be gone two days?" Abigail wondered what she would do rattling around in this house for two days, but before any thoughts could evolve, Desh said, "Now, Abigail, I don't want you taking matters into your own hands while I'm gone. I want you to stay in this house, so that nobody will see you, and so I'll know you're safe. Will you promise me that?"

"Desh, I—"

"Please, Abigail, if you don't promise me, I'll worry myself to death while I'm gone. I just want to know you're okay while I'm not here to watch out for you."

"Desh, we've been over this. You can't let me and my problems take over your life! And I can't wait around for you to hold my hand every moment of the day. But I promise you that whatever I do, I'll be careful."

"I don't like the sound of that! What are you planning on doing in the next couple of days that can't wait until I get home?"

"I haven't made any plans. Remember, I didn't know you were going anywhere. All I'm saying is, *if* I decide to do something, I'll be careful. But, really, what can I do? You have the key to the passageway to my house, and I assume you're taking your car. And I don't think I can drive your pickup since it's a standard transmission. So that pretty much leaves me stranded, doesn't it?" Abigail couldn't keep a tinge of resentment from her voice.

"Abigail, you have to understand how concerned I am

about you. You didn't know your enemies that well when you lived here. You probably didn't even know you *had* enemies until you were framed for killing your dad. Then you were away for ten years, and didn't know what was going on in this town. Well, I've been here. I've been listening, watching, and asking questions, and these people are not playing games. They mean business. And I'm talking dirty business, if that's what it takes for them to get what they want."

"But you said they wouldn't burn my house until they found the will. By the same token, I don't believe they'll try to kill me until they get the information they want from me. They probably think I know where it is, so they won't kill me, yet."

"They killed your dad before they got the information from him." Desh's harsh reasoning shot Abigail's theory down.

"But they thought they could get me to sell."

"Well, if you're dead, your property will go to the state, then it will be open to any buyer. As far as they know it would be better for them if you were dead. I haven't wanted to frighten you with the obvious, but if it takes that to make you understand why I'm so concerned about you, then there, you have it!"

Finally the magnitude of the situation sank in for Abigail. He was right. If she were dead, as far as they knew, her enemies' problems would be over.

She opened her mouth to answer, but no words came out.

Desh took her hands and pulled her to him. "I'm sorry, baby. I didn't want to scare you. I don't want to go to jail, like you did, but if anybody hurts you, I'll kill every son-of-a-bitch in this town that I think is part of this mess. So, I'm trying to protect myself, as well as you."

"Why, Desh? Why have you taken on this case so passionately? I'm nothing to you."

"Abigail Avery, you're *everything* to me. Haven't you

figured that out yet? You're the only woman I've ever loved. I vowed when I saw them take you away that I'd find out who did this to you. I vowed that I'd make them pay. I'd planned to follow in my dad's footsteps and become a coach and teacher until the day I saw Sheriff Lucas cram you into the back seat of that patrol car and drive away with you. On that day, I decided to become a lawyer so I'd be able to legally take these people down.

"I love you, Abigail. I've loved you since the first day I saw you at school, in your ragged little dress, standing and watching the other kids play. I wanted to protect you then, and I still want to protect you. I'll go to my death protecting you, if that's what it takes." He wrapped his arms around he, pulling her close.

"I'll be leaving very early in the morning, before you wake up." He stepped back to look into her eyes. "I expect you to be here safe and sound when I get back." He dropped a brief kiss on her lips and left the room.

Abigail sat back on the side of her bed, too stunned to think. Her brain couldn't seem to absorb all that had been said in the brief few minutes since Desh had walked into the room.

But two things were sure. She was in real danger and Desh honestly seemed to love her. She could understand the danger much easier than she could understand the love. She knew danger. She had no concept of love.

And one other thing. She hadn't promised Desh that she'd stay in the house. If there was this much danger, then she needed to get this thing solved before Desh got too involved and ruined his life.

Chapter 11

Dawn was just breaking as Abigail awakened the next morning to the wakeup call of Rambo Rooster, as she'd started calling him. This morning she welcomed his wakeup call. She wanted to get her day started early, hopefully before anyone else was up and prowling.

The house was quiet as Abigail made her way down the stairs. She could tell by the empty feel of the house that Desh wasn't there. For the first time since her mom died, she actually missed someone. Yet another new and strange sensation.

She grabbed a quick breakfast and headed out the front door. It wasn't a very long walk to her place, but it would be best to do it in the early morning before the day started heating up.

She'd lain awake last night trying to come up with a way to get to her house. The only way she could think of was to walk on the public road until she was almost there, then cut through the woods to get to her place. She couldn't take the chance of actually walking up the driveway to her house and being seen.

A vague memory of her mom and her cutting through the woods and walking to the Draper place led her on. She was sure there used to be an old log road or some kind of trail that went from the public road to the back of her property. Well—Desh's property, she reminded herself. It probably had grown over with underbrush by now, but maybe there would be a way for her to get through.

It was going to be a hot, humid Mississippi day. Even this early in the morning the humidity caused her skin to feel clammy and uncomfortable. Her clothes already tried to cling to her damp body.

But the heat and humidity couldn't put a damper on the beauty that surrounded her. Early sunlight filtered through the treetops, reflecting prisms of light off the dewdrops that still clung to the leaves and grass. Birds called to each other from tall trees that, in places, formed a natural tunnel over the country road.

Once again, the thrill of being free from prison shot through Abigail. This is what she'd missed the most—the elements. Nature. Birds singing. Wind blowing through her hair. The sun shining on her upturned face. Walking in the rain. These had been Abigail's playmates as a lonely child. Just knowing she could enjoy these things no matter where she lived, comforted her.

As she walked, she watched for any sign or feeling of familiarity of the spot where the old cut-through should be. She was beginning to lose hope when she spotted an old, rusted iron gate barely visible from the road.

She'd worn her only pair of jeans and her "sturdy" shoes from prison, but the briars and underbrush still clawed and held on to her legs as if trying to hold her back from her journey. Occasionally a thorn made its way through the fabric of her pants and pricked her skin, but she paid no attention to the sharp pain as she eagerly approached the old gate.

She was disappointed to find it too overgrown to open. She'd just have to climb over it. Even though it wobbled and groaned, Abigail was soon on the other side. As she dropped to the ground and looked around, she realized the tall grove of pine trees that lay before her had smothered out most of the undergrowth. Cool shade and pine needles invited her to continue her journey. Immediately she spotted what appeared to be old ruts and uneven places that gave credence to her memory of the log road.

Smiling at her progress, Abigail followed the vague outline of the old road, and in no time saw the silhouette of her barn coming into view. She was in the "woods" that her dad had always warned her to stay out of. The woods that she'd been taught to be afraid of were, indeed, a beautiful haven.

Somewhere close was the opening to the cave, but she didn't have time to look for it. Right now she needed to get to the house without being seen by anyone who might already be watching the place.

Staying in the shadows as much as possible, Abigail quickly made her way to the back of the house. Once inside the screened back porch, she inhaled a deep breath of relief, then stood immobile and listened for any signs of movement from the inside or outside. All was quiet, so she continued into the kitchen.

Now what? Why had it been so important for her to come here today? What was she looking for? Was she just trying to prove to Desh that she could come here if she wanted to? If there wasn't a deed to look for, were there some other clues that she could find?

Not daring to turn on any lights, Abigail waited for her eyes to adjust to the dim interior. Dusty shadows and vague memories engulfed her. It was as if she'd never left. She almost expected her father to yell at her from somewhere in the house.

Sudden anger flooded Abigail. Anger toward her father for everything he'd ever done to her. Anger at her mother for being such a weak woman that she would allow her child to be raised in such conditions. Anger at her grandparents for being too stubborn to even try to see their grandchild. And deep, bitter anger for a town that had stolen ten years of her young life.

Which brought her back to her father. He was the one, after all, who'd caused all of this. If he hadn't been such a loser, none of this would have happened.

Overcome with emotions that had been bottled up for too long, Abigail had to do something. She might not be able to burn that hated recliner where he'd passed out every night, but she could sure as hell destroy it!

Returning to the back porch, she went to a corner where she knew a crowbar would be leaning against the wall. Why her father insisted on keeping a crowbar in this particular corner, she never knew. She'd never seen him use it. But today, *she'd* make good use of it.

She thrilled as her hands wrapped around the cold metal shaft. Years of pent up fury exploded from Abigail Avery as she made her way back to the living room. The first lick from the heavy tool whacked solidly on the spot where her father's head had lolled each night after he'd fallen into a drunken sleep.

The solid sound of the crowbar whacking the old chair unleashed a life's worth of wrath that Abigail had been containing all these years. She lost control of time as she pounded, jabbed and pulverized the chair symbolizing everyone who'd ever hurt her.

As the haze of rage slowly lifted, Abigail stood weak and exhausted, the crowbar hanging loosely from her hands. She gazed at the crumpled old recliner. Its broken pieces lay scattered on the floor. The seat still clung haphazardly to the back of the chair, so Abigail used her last remaining strength and kicked at it. She didn't want one single part of that dreaded chair clinging to another part. She wanted it totally disintegrated.

As the back of the chair reluctantly let go of the seat and finished falling to the floor, a large manila envelope slid out of the hiding place where it had rested, undetected, for years.

The sight of the envelope finished clearing Abigail's head. Knowing she'd found something significant, she was almost afraid to pick the envelope up. It was heavier than it looked, and bulky.

Is this what everyone is looking for? she wondered.

Suddenly afraid that she'd get caught with the package before she could examine it, she cautiously looked out of all the windows to make sure nobody was around. She *had* to get back to Desh's place undetected. She must not panic! She eased out the back door of the house, moving slowly, hoping not to attract any attention if anyone was watching the house. She hugged the shadows of the house and barn as much as possible until she was safely hidden in the tall pine trees.

Weak with relief that she'd made it this far, she wondered if she should hide the package in the cave and wait until Desh got home, or take a chance of getting caught with it while walking on the road back to the his place.

No! She couldn't wait for Desh to get home. She had to know what was in the package. With the decision made, she continued back through the woods.

Once on the road back to Desh's place, she hugged the package to her body and listened intently for any approaching vehicle. If she heard a vehicle approaching, she'd jump into the closest clump of bushes and hide.

The sun was fully up now. Sweat beaded on Abigail's forehead as she hurried along. The walk back seemed to take twice as long as the trip this morning had. But finally she saw the house coming into view. She ran the rest of the way and was soon safely inside the cool living room. Locking the door behind her, she ran up the stairs to her room.

Her hands trembled as she unfastened the clasp holding the envelope closed. Taking a deep breath to steady her nerves, Abigail slowly dumped the contents of the package onto her bed. She watched in awe as packets of one hundred dollar bills slid out. She picked a packet up and counted ten bills. So each packet represented a thousand dollars. In amazement, she counted fifty packets. Fifty thousand dollars? She'd been raised in poverty while her dad literally sat on fifty thousand dollars? Had he slowly accrued the money, or had he been paid off for something he'd done just before his death? Was that why someone wanted him dead? Or had he robbed a bank?

Abigail sat on the side of her bed holding several packets of the money. Her head was beginning to ache. It seemed that the more she found out, the more questions she had. Would she ever get to the bottom of this mystery?

She opened the envelope to put the money back, but the first packet hung on something and wouldn't go in. Looking inside, she found a folded document that felt like several sheets of paper. Now what?

Opening the papers, she was amazed to discover several elaborate drawings. Fine details etched on the paper showed circles and lines and things that didn't make any sense to Abigail. Had her father done this? Was the money payment for these drawings? But what were they?

After studying the drawings for several minutes, she finally shoved them back into the envelope with the money. She'd just have to wait until Desh got home. Maybe he'd have some idea of what she'd found.

But she was convinced this was an important find. She felt sure this was what the entire hullabaloo was about. It might tie in with the deed to her place, but this appeared to be much more important than the deed.

Feeling the need to hide the envelope, she crammed it under her mattress. Not that she thought anyone would be in Desh's house snooping around, but suddenly she was paranoid, just knowing what she had in her possession.

Loud pounding on the front door startled Abigail. Who on earth could that be? She hastened down the stairs and peered out the curtains to see Mabelle Henley nervously glancing around.

"Is anyone home?" Mabelle called, just as Abigail opened the door. "Thank goodness!" she exclaimed, and rushed in.

"Mabelle, what's wrong?" Abigail could see the woman was agitated.

"They know you're back!" she said, plopping down in the closest chair.

"How do you know?"

"I heard Judge Haney and Sheriff Lucas talking about it in Ma Tucker's. I came out here as soon as I heard what they said. I didn't see Desh's car, so I was afraid you'd be gone, too. I'm so glad you're here! Where's Desh?"

"He took his dad to Birmingham. They'll be back tomorrow," Abigail said, then regretted telling too much. "But what did you hear, Mabelle?"

"Judge Haney said he'd just gotten a call from someone who'd been watching the house. They'd seen someone slinking from your house this morning. They couldn't tell who it was, but said it moved like a woman! Judge Haney told Sheriff Lucas that it had to be you. That he knew you were back, he just couldn't figure out where you're staying. Were you there, Abigail?"

"No. As you can see, I don't have a vehicle, so I've been right here." Abigail's sudden distrust of Mabelle surprised her. But for some reason she felt like Mabelle was digging for information.

"You could have walked," Mabelle persisted.

"Who do *you* think was there?" Abigail asked.

"How should I know? I don't have a clue. I just wanted to let you know that Judge Haney thinks you're back, so you should be very careful." She seemed totally genuine in her concern, causing a flash of guilt to run through Abigail. "It's a good thing you got fat while you were away. That'll sure help keep people from recognizing you."

"You recognized me," Abigail replied, very much aware of the emphasis that Mabelle put on *fat*.

"It was your eyes and hair. Those were your two trademark features. Since your hair is different, I don't think people will be as quick to recognize your eyes." Mabelle paused, then asked, "Are you in love with Desh?"

"What?"

"Are you in love with Desh?" Mabelle repeated.

"Why would you ask me something like that? What has that got to do with what we're talking about, anyway?"

"It's nothing to do with what we're talking about. I just need to know."

"Why do you need to know, Mabelle? You've already warned me to stay away from him. In the restaurant you didn't seem to care if I loved him or not. You just told me he was yours. So why do you care if I love him?"

"Half the women in this town are in love with him, whether they'll admit it or not. You have to admit he's sexy as any actor you've ever seen."

"Are you really in love with him?" Abigail asked.

"Yes. I've been in love with him since school. That's why I've never married. I keep waiting, thinking he'll realize I'm the woman he loves."

"Have you ever told him?"

"Of course not!"

"Then how's he going to know? If you love him so much, you need to let him know, don't you?"

"I have my ways of letting him know. He'll get the message some day. That is, if you don't try to interfere. But I really don't think I have anything to worry about. I truly don't think he'd be attracted to someone your size. Desh seems like the kind of guy who'd like little women like me."

Was this woman being mean, or did she just feel that she was stating the obvious? Abigail couldn't figure out how to take Mabelle. One minute she seemed really concerned about her, then the next minute she seemed to be subtly putting her down. Was she friend or foe?

Desh's declaration of his love for her popped into Abigail's mind, causing a tiny smile to toy with her lips. Wonder how Mabelle would react if she told her how wrong she was? Or was Desh just saying those things to make her feel better about herself?

Whatever. Abigail wasn't about to get into a fight over Desh Elliot with Mabelle. "Well, Mabelle, if you came here today to find out my intentions toward Desh, you can relax. I don't have any plans to become Mrs. Desh Elliot." Even as Abigail said the words, she felt excitement at the thought. But knew how impossible it would be. Desh Elliot would never marry an ex-convict, no matter what size she was. He deserved better than that.

"I hope not, Abigail. Because while I will do all I can to help you bring down the people who killed your dad and sent you to prison, I'd sure be your enemy if you tried to steal Desh from me!"

So that was it! Mabelle was friend *and* foe! No. Not friend. Maybe ally, but not friend. Not in the real sense of the word. That's why she didn't mind shooting the little zingers about her weight at Abigail. Friends don't deliberately try to make you feel like less of a person.

"Well, Mabelle, I can't steal something from you that you don't even have, can I?"

"Just be careful, Abigail. As much as I hate Judge Haney and want to see him brought down, I'll only do so much to help you, if you cross me."

"Mabelle, why are you threatening me? Since when did I become your enemy? The night you did my hair, you said I'd turned into a beautiful woman. You said you'd always be my friend because I helped you with Ned Thompson. But since then, you've made several unkind references to me about being fat. You said you'd always be my friend, and now you're threatening me. What's up, Mabelle?" Abigail felt herself slipping back into the self-protection mode she'd had to use in prison. Something just wasn't right, here.

"Well, I said those things before I realized you were planning to move in and live with Desh. You *are* a beautiful woman, even if you're fat. And I will always remember and appreciate you taking up for me. But—you know the old saying, 'All's fair in love and war.' I guess I'm just warning you that I'll fight for Desh, no matter what the circumstances."

"I don't think you have anything to worry about," Abigail assured her. Not that she wanted to reassure Mabelle. But common sense told her that Abigail Avery had no future with Desh Elliot.

"So, did you come here today to warn me about Judge Haney or Desh?"

"I came to tell you that they know you're back. But I took the opportunity to talk with you about Desh."

"Did you tell me everything you heard the men talking about? Is there more I should know?"

"There was one other thing. Judge Haney told Sheriff Lucas to find you and bring you in on any charges he could come up with, and they'd *figure out* a way to get you to sell your property. The way he said it sounded really scary, Abigail."

"Desh said you really hate Judge Haney. Why?"

"I got my reasons. And I think I've got proof of something

to really hurt him."

"Mabelle! What? Tell me!"

"Not yet. For my own protection, I've got to wait until I see what you're going to do. How far you're going to get with your revenge. If I accuse him of what he's done with nothing else to back me up, I could kiss my life goodbye in this town. Maybe altogether." A flash of fear crossed her face. "I'll let you and Desh in on my secret when I think it's safe for me."

Before Abigail could say anything else, Mabelle turned and ran from the porch to her car and sped away.

Chapter 12

Stunned, Abigail watched Mabelle's car disappear down the road. She had to find a way to get that information from Mabelle. She hoped it was the same as her own. If so, they'd have Judge Haney right where they needed him. That would be the first one on her list taken care of. Even though she wanted to save him until last, she'd take him down when and however she could.

She made a quick sandwich and glass of iced tea and went back to her room. While eating, she mulled over the drawings from the envelope. What were they? They made no sense. But as she studied them a small nudging began to form in her mind. Something seemed familiar.

Turning the drawings one way, then another, Abigail tried to understand what they could be. Two small dots on one of the pages were the only things that might indicate anything in particular. But were they just accidental spots that had gotten on the page? Everything else was circles and lines.

Finally tossing them onto the bed, she carried her plate

and glass back to the kitchen and washed her dishes. So what was she going to do with the rest of the day and tomorrow? She hated being stranded like this. Although, she had to admit, she'd made a good bit of progress this morning.

The house and barn. The thought stopped Abigail in her tracks. Rushing back upstairs, she grabbed the paper with the two dots on them. Everything on the page fell into perspective. The two dots represented her house and barn. The drawings were of the caves that led from her house to Desh's. She recognized everything Desh had shown her. Even the side room where her dad's moonshine still was. So the other pages had to represent additional cave systems someone had drawn.

Placing the pages in different positions, Abigail soon realized they were like puzzle pieces. Once she fit the matching lines of the edges together, she had the layout of a network of caverns that ended on the last page with one huge circle, which she assumed represented a large underground room.

Someone had spent a long time drawing this underground map. But why? And why was it in her dad's old chair in an envelope full of money?

Frustration filled Abigail. She hated having to wait for Desh to get home to further explore this. Hated the feeling that she couldn't act on her own.

It was too late today to do anything else, but tomorrow—tomorrow she'd do some more exploring, she promised herself. Desh said he wouldn't be home until late, so she'd have time to make a little progress.

The sharp ringing of the phone caught Abigail's attention. She rushed to it, hoping it would be Desh. *Why would she hope that?* The little warning signal went unheeded as she listened to his voice tell the caller to leave a message. If it was him, she'd pick up.

"Desh, this is Judge Haney." Abigail would have recognized his hated voice anywhere. "Is Abigail Avery staying with you?

We need to know right away. Someone has ransacked her house, and we need to find out who it was. Call me."

Maybe I should have picked up and told him it was me, Abigail thought. So they had discovered the chair. Which meant they went into her house at will. Resentment filled her. Did they really think they could just take over her property without a fight? Did they think she would roll over and play dead and let them have it? Well, they had another thought coming! And she was sick and tired of waiting around for Desh to decide to do something. Tomorrow, she would make a move.

It was time they knew Abigail Avery was back. It was time they knew she was totally different from the innocent young girl they'd sent to prison.

She was about to settle in for the night when the phone rang again. This time it was Desh. "Abigail, pick up if you can hear me," he said to the machine.

Abigail quickly grabbed the phone and said, "Hi, Desh, I'm here."

"Good! I was hoping you'd answer. Are you okay?"

"Sure. Why do you ask?"

"You sound different. Excited, or something. Are you sure nothing is wrong?

"I'm fine, Desh," she answered.

"Well, okay. I'm not convinced, but I guess I have to take your word for it. Listen, the doctors want to keep Dad a couple more days to run some tests. They think they may have his blood too thin, so they want to watch him while they try to adjust his medicine. It will be several days before I get back. I hate to leave you stranded at the house alone, but try to amuse yourself, if you can. I know you're anxious to get on with our investigation, but just be patient until I get home."

"Your first priority is your dad, Desh. Don't worry about me. I'll be fine. I'll find something to amuse myself, like you suggested." She hoped she sounded convincing.

After insisting she take the phone numbers to the hospital and his hotel room, Desh reluctantly got off the phone.

He couldn't shake the feeling that something was wrong with Abigail. Her voice was different. He'd love to believe it was because she was excited to hear from him, but it was more than that. Much more.

Maybe he'd go home tomorrow and come back for his dad when the doctors released him. His dad slept most of the time, anyway. That, or watched TV. There really wasn't any reason for him to stay, other than the long drive back and forth. He'd talk with the doctors and his dad in the morning and make his decision.

The next morning, Abigail called Mabelle. "Mabelle, I hate to bother you at work, but I need a way into town. I need to buy a car. Is there any way you can come and get me? I'll pay you for the gas to drive out here."

"Sure, Abigail." Mabelle sounded friendly and agreeable this morning. "I'll be out there as soon as I finish my nine o'clock appointment. It'll probably be a little after ten when I get there."

Mabelle sounded totally different than she had when they'd talked the day before. Abigail felt as if she might get whiplash just trying to keep up with the woman's mood swings.

Wondering briefly if she was doing the right thing, Abigail counted out five thousand dollars from the stash in the envelope. After all, it was hers. It was her dad's, and it was left in her house. That made it hers, didn't it?

Her reasoning made perfect sense to her, so she crammed the money into her purse and waited impatiently for Mabelle. *It was left in Desh's house,* a small voice reminded her. "But it was my dad's chair," she said loudly to the voice.

While she waited for Mabelle, Abigail went to the phone.

She'd realized last night that Desh had Caller ID on the phone. She scrolled down the list of callers until she found Judge Haney's number and wrote it down. A slight smile lifted the corners of her mouth as she put the phone number into her wallet.

"Just take me to Tucker's Used But Not Abused car lot," Abigail said, getting into Mabelle's Ford Mustang when she finally arrived.

"Abigail, if you don't mind me asking, how are you going to buy a car?"

"I'll get a loan," Abigail hedged.

"From Dan Tucker? Do you think he'll give a stranger in town a car loan? He's real hard-boiled when it comes to his precious cars. And *real* hard-boiled if you don't pay your notes on time. He'll send his goons out to repossess the vehicle if a person gets one week behind on his payments."

"Maybe I'll just tell him who I am," Abigail said.

"Are you crazy? He was one of the jurors on your trial, wasn't he?" Mabelle fairly screeched. "And I thought Desh wanted you to stay in hiding for now."

"He does. And you're right. I'm not going to tell Dan Tucker who I am. I'll be Mary Draper for now," Abigail assured her as Mabelle pulled up in front of the car lot.

Abigail felt her insides quiver a little as Dan Tucker, himself, approached her.

"Good morning!" he said in his best "reel this sucker in" voice. "How may I help you this morning? Are you looking for anything in particular?" By now, he had Abigail's hand in his, pumping it up and down. He hadn't changed a lot in the ten years since she'd last seen him sitting in the jury, looking bored and sleepy. He still looked bored and sleepy, but his voice remained alert and friendly.

She relaxed, realizing that he had no clue who she was. "I need to look around a little," she said. "I'm looking for something real inexpensive for now."

"Oh." She could hear the disappointment in his voice. "Jim, come and help this lady find a car," he called to a young man sitting in a side office.

After letting Jim show her around, Abigail settled on a 1998 Honda with high mileage and bad tires. But the price tag was good. A thousand dollars.

Since she was paying cash, Jim wrote out a bill of sale to Mary Draper at the fake address in a neighboring town that Abigail gave him.

Now if she could just avoid getting stopped by a policeman, she'd be okay. She'd probably wind up back in jail if they stopped her with no driver's license or insurance. But that was a chance she had to take right now. She'd worry about all that stuff later.

Probably not the usual car a Realtor would drive, Abigail admitted, glancing around the worn interior of the old car. But, hopefully, it wouldn't draw a lot of attention to her either.

Her first stop was a pay phone. Her hands trembled as she dialed Judge Haney's home phone number. She hoped against hope she'd get his answering machine. After four rings his voice came on the machine instructing the caller to leave a detailed message. "The end is near," she whispered into the receiver and hung up.

Her next stop was the garage that had belonged to Jim Duncan before he died. She pulled her little car in between two huge trucks that were there to have repairs done on them, parked, and went inside.

"Who owns this garage?" she asked the receptionist, a middle-aged, slightly graying woman who looked totally bored.

"Josh Duncan. Why do you ask?"

"Is he around?" Abigail asked.

"He's never around. He owns the place, but he's never

wanted it. He inherited it from his dad, but he could care less about it."

"Then why doesn't he sell it?"

"Because his uncle, Harry Haney, uses this place to keep all his tire-hauling trucks running. I think he actually pays Josh to keep the place open. He's sure not making any money from anyone else. Nobody else comes here."

"So I can't get new tires for my car?" Abigail asked.

"Nope. You'll have to go over to Thompson's Tire Shop to do that."

She headed for Thompson's Tire Shop. This was even better. She'd use the excuse of new tires to snoop around the Thompsons' place a little. Since three of the jurors were from this one shop, maybe they had more invested in her situation than some of the others.

A young man with greasy hands and clothes greeted her. She told him she needed new tires all around.

"You want to wait while we do it, ma'am? We ain't that busy today, so we can get right on it."

"That would be great," Abigail said.

"You can wait inside if you want to."

Abigail thanked him and entered the dingy, smoke-filled office. Her luck was holding. She could snoop around while she waited for the tires to be put on her car.

Nobody was in the front office, but she could hear a man's voice in a back room. She couldn't understand what he was saying, but he sounded agitated. Angry.

Glancing around, she saw a "Restrooms" sign and decided to take advantage of the facility while she waited. Almost afraid of what she'd find, she hesitantly opened the door to the small restroom and peered inside. She was surprised to find it relatively clean.

As she closed the door behind her, she realized she could distinctly hear the man on the phone. And his words

Pat Ballard

immobilized her.

"I'm tellin' you, Judge Haney, if we don't get access to that other entrance soon, and I mean *damn* soon, we're going to have to stop taking tires. Either that, or we have to start burning tires. I know you don't want to do that because it might bring attention to your operation, but you have to make the choice. My entrance is getting so clogged, it's almost impossible to get the trucks through there."

Silence as he listened to the voice on the other end of the phone.

"Well, you'd better find her. Or figure out how to get that place of hers without her. One way or the other, we have to have the entrance that's on her property. Or I'm tellin' you our operation is going to shut down. Time's runnin' out, Judge," he fairly yelled. He hung up the phone with a bang.

"Stupid old sonofabitch," Abigail heard him mumble, before a squeaking chair indicated he was getting up.

Oh, great, she thought. If he discovered she'd been in the restroom, he'd know she overheard him.

She heard shuffling footsteps pass the restroom door. Soon he could be heard in the garage yelling obscenities at the workers.

Now, if she could get back into the front office and get outside without him seeing her, maybe he'd never suspect she'd heard him.

Luck was with her as she made her way to the front door and eased around the building in the opposite direction of where the guys were working on her tires. She'd say she was just looking around, if they discovered her on this side of the building.

She was intrigued, as she came around the corner of the building, to see the flat, ivy-covered wall of a tall bank rising up behind the garage. She hadn't realized there was a hill behind the garage. And nestled in the thick ivy were two huge wooden

128

doors that obviously covered the entrance to—what? Could there possibly be a cave entrance here? It almost looked as if the ivy was there to camouflage the doors.

"Whut the hell you doin' back here?"

Abigail whirled to look into the older, bleary blue eyes of Ned Thompson. The voice on the phone.

"And who the hell are you? I ain't never seen you in these parts before. Tim said you's gettin' new tires on. You passin' through?"

Relief flooded Abigail that he didn't recognize her.

"I'm Mary Draper," Abigail said. "I'm in town for a few weeks looking for some property for a client." It had worked on Judge Haney; surely it would work on Ned Thompson.

She watched suspicion wash over his face, but before he could say anything, the young mechanic rounded the corner. "Your car's ready, ma'am," he said.

"Boy, don't you see we're talkin,' here?" Ned yelled at him.

"No, we're finished," Abigail said, heading to the front of the building.

She quickly paid her bill and was about to get into the car when a hand on her arm stopped her. Startled, she snatched her arm away.

"My, my. You sure are jumpy." Ned Thompson was so close she smelled his stale tobacco breath. "I don't think you're who you say you are, Mary Draper. There ain't no property around here to be bought. Only one place, and it ain't for sale." He chuckled nastily. "Well, it is, but not to no outsiders. So you might as well go on back home. Where did you say? Oh, yeah, you said a 'neighboring town,' didn't you. That's kind of vague, don't you think?"

Abigail didn't like the conversation at all, so she sat down in her car and closed the door. But Ned leaned down into the open window. "I think I'll have Sheriff Lucas run a check on

Miss Mary Draper. Is it Miss or Mrs.? Wonder what he'll find." And he stood up and slapped the side of her car as he walked off.

Abigail's ears were throbbing from her pounding heart. Ned Thompson was going to be trouble. It was too early in the game for trouble. He'd start asking questions, and things might come to a head before she collected all the information she needed.

And Judge Haney had called Desh's house, so he was already connecting her to Desh. She had to get away from that house. Had to find a place to stay so they wouldn't suspect Desh of being involved with her. That would really hurt him in this town.

Thank goodness, she'd found that money in her dad's chair. She'd go back to Desh's place, get the money and her things and find a place to stay. Maybe she'd even go to Smith's Hollow, about twenty miles from here, and rent a room. She could drive back and forth, to do her investigating in Leaky Springs.

Feeling better about her new plan, her heart rate began to settle down a little. In fact, she was anxious to get her things and get away from Dashing Desh Elliot. She just couldn't think straight when she was around him. She was too aware of him when he was in the room with her. She acted differently around him than she had ever done around anyone. This side of her was a stranger. Someone she never knew existed.

She wanted to let him take care of her when he was around. Wanted to bask in the light flashing in his beautiful green eyes when he smiled at her. Wanted to let him touch her when he reached for her. And she wanted to believe that he loved her, like he said he did.

But nobody had ever loved Abigail Avery. So she knew she couldn't trust the feelings of this stranger inside her. She had to rely and depend on the Abigail Avery who'd always had to fend for her own self.

Yes, it was time to get away from Desh Elliot.

"Hello, Abigail, I'm home," Desh called as he opened the front door. A grin spread across his face. That felt really right. He could picture himself coming home every day saying that.

He listened for her response, or some noise in the house to indicate where she was. But total quietness answered him.

"Abigail, where are you?" he called.

Nothing.

Maybe she was in her room taking a nap. It was the middle of the afternoon, but she may have gotten bored. He decided to check his messages before going upstairs to find her.

The only message on his machine was that of Judge Harry Haney. After listening to the message a couple of times, Desh bounded up the stairs. He had to talk with Abigail to see if she knew what was going on. Surely she hadn't gone to her place while he was away.

After knocking on her door and not getting an answer, he opened it to find an empty room. The bed was neatly made and everything in its place.

But no Abigail.

Chapter 13

Abigail was dismayed to see Desh's car sitting in the yard when she got to the house. He said he'd be gone a few more days. Well, she'd just have to tell him her plans. She was sure he'd understand.

She opened the door to hear her name being bellowed throughout the house. It seemed to originate from upstairs and reverberate throughout the house as it eerily bounced off the walls. Was something wrong with Desh? Had he hurt himself?

She tossed her purse on the closest chair and headed for the stairs. Just then Desh roared her name again and bounded down the stairs. He stopped abruptly when he saw her.

"Where the hell were you?" he asked, coming toward her again.

"I just got home."

"From where? How did you go anywhere? Did you walk?" He bombarded her with questions so fast she couldn't answer.

But before she even tried, he pulled her into his arms and crushed her to his chest. "Oh, Abigail. I heard the message from Judge Haney, then I couldn't find you and I was going crazy! I thought they'd taken you from me again." His voice sounded strained and choked, filled with emotions she didn't understand.

Abigail tried to pull back to look at him, but he held her close. "No, stay here for a moment. Let me feel you. Let me know you're really here in my arms."

So she relaxed and just for the moment gloried in the sense of safety his strong arms always brought to her. How would it be to know this feeling was hers to keep? To get used to? To expect?

Before she could explore her thoughts, she felt his lips softly kissing the curve of her neck, then working their way along her jawline before claiming her own. And for the first time, she didn't resist. She gave as much as she received. Leaning into him, she parted her lips for him. Wrapped her arms around him to pull him closer.

His kiss deepened, grew more heated, more intense, as he sensed her response. Their breathing became one as they inhaled each other's expelled breath. Nothing had ever excited Abigail as this did. She felt herself growing weak and languid, yet her pulses were racing as if she'd run a mile. She didn't understand what was happening to her, but she didn't care. This was too wonderful to stop. *Please don't stop,* she silently begged.

But Desh had to stop while he still could. The dull ache in his lower body reminded him that he was losing control.

Abigail's soft moan as he pulled his lips from hers shot a thrill of excitement through him. She didn't want to stop, and that meant more to him than anything she could have done. Gave him hope that he'd been afraid to have.

"Abigail, as much as I want to continue this, we have to talk," he said, sitting on the couch and pulling her down beside him. "Now talk to me."

Abigail wondered how she could concentrate with him this close. With his arm on the back of the couch, practically encircling her shoulders. With his other hand still holding one of hers. And with his beautiful green eyes gazing deeply into hers. Her awareness of Desh Elliot had rapidly escalated to new levels. She wanted to feel his lips on hers again. Wanted to run her hands through that unruly blond hair and feel it twine around her fingers. Wanted to feel his hands—

Suddenly needing distance so she could think, she tried to take her hand from his and move away. But he stopped her. "No. Stay close, Abigail. I need to feel you close to me. I need to soak you in. Now please tell me what's going on."

So Abigail told him everything she'd done since he'd been gone, and ended with her intentions to leave the house so he wouldn't be connected to her.

When she'd finished, Desh just sat and stared at her, momentarily too stunned to speak. Finally he said, "Abigail, I don't know where to start! You've endangered yourself on so many fronts that I'm speechless."

"Aren't you making this a little more dramatic than it is, Desh? I mean, after all, these people don't even recognize me. And all I did was go to my own house and destroy an old chair, then I bought a car and got tires for it. Now how dangerous can that be?"

"Don't play innocent with me. If you weren't concerned, you wouldn't be talking about leaving this house to protect me. So, I'll just start there. You can't leave here."

"Excuse me?" Abigail quickly stood up and faced Desh. "All of my life someone has told me where to go, what to do and how to do it. I'm a free woman, Desh. For the first time in my life, I'm *free*. So while I appreciate what you're trying to do for me, I'm not going to let you tell me where I can and can't go."

"Abigail, please sit down. I think it's time I told you the

whole truth about the people you're dealing with." Concern edged Desh's voice. He still wasn't sure it was safe for her to know everything. But at the rate she was going, she was bound to be in more danger by not knowing.

Abigail saw the serious look on Desh's face and sat in a nearby chair. She wasn't about to sit back on the couch beside him. She couldn't think straight when he was that close.

"When you were sent away I decided to go to law school to learn as much as I could about the law, so that when you came home I could help you get your revenge on the people who sent you to prison.

"After I graduated I set up an office in the courthouse. I wanted to be in the middle of everything that went on so I could keep my ears and eyes open for anything that wasn't on the up and up.

"It's amazing what I was able to hear by just sitting in my office and listening to conversations in the hallway, or even in other offices when they left their doors open.

"Also, I made it my habit to hang out in the same places Judge Haney and his friends frequented. Which, as you know, in Leaky Springs, there aren't that many options, so it didn't look real conspicuous when I happened to be in all the right places.

"Anyway, it didn't take me long to keep picking up on one general thread of conversation. Judge Haney seemed to talk to a lot of people about his "waste tire business." But it was always talked about in a hush-hush tone of voice, so I started getting suspicious that this business he had on the side might not be legal. I knew I couldn't be obvious, but I started asking questions, and nobody seemed to know anything about it. I didn't ask obvious people, like the Thompsons, because I knew if they were involved with the judge, they'd tell him I was snooping.

"After not getting anywhere in Leaky Springs, I started

going to the surrounding towns and asking questions. That's when I began to hit the jackpot. It appears that Judge Haney has a fairly large waste tire disposal service going on. Most of the small gas stations that sell, change or repair tires let his trucks pick up their tires and dispose of them.

"So my next question was how was he disposing of them? I couldn't find any record of him acquiring a license or permit from the state to operate this business. Nor could I find an established place where he did his recycling, which is required if you have a business like this.

"In the middle of my research, about a year ago, I was approached by someone from the Environmental Protection Agency, asking if I'd be interested in helping them track down someone who was running an illegal dumping operation. It seems that someone had told the Agency I'd been asking questions. Of course I agreed to help them, and have been working with them ever since.

"Abigail, this is top secret stuff. You can't breath a word that I'm telling you. And I'm only telling you this because I'm afraid you're getting in too deep with your own investigating efforts. You and I are both in real danger, here."

"So you think them wanting my property is connected to Judge Haney's illegal tire dumping business?"

"I'm pretty sure it is. I became suspicious early on that he might be using the caves to dump in, but I couldn't find any entrances that were large enough to dump tires into. I'd about given up on that idea until you said you heard trucks during the night. When we heard them in the cave the other night, I realized that I'm very close to finding out the information I need. I just need to find out where they're entering the caves with the trucks."

"Well, I might be able to shed some light on that, after today," Abigail offered, remembering the two huge doors that seemed to open right into the side of the mountain behind the Thompsons' service station. She'd failed to mention that to Desh when she was relaying her day to him.

"What?" he questioned eagerly.

"After I heard Ned on the phone, I didn't want him to know I'd been in the restroom because he'd have surely known I could hear his conversation from there, so I went out the front door and went to the opposite side of the building from where they were working, to make him think I'd been back there looking around instead of inside the station. On the opposite side of the station from where they do their service work is a sharp knoll that's covered in English ivy. And nestled in that ivy are two huge doors that look like they open right into the side of the hill. You could drive just about any size vehicle into that opening."

"That's it! You wonderful woman! You've found our answer!" Desh pulled Abigail from her chair and wrapped her in a bear hug.

Laughing at his excitement, Abigail pushed back from him. "Desh, there's more. I think you should see what I found in my dad's old chair."

"What do you mean she discovered the doors?" Judge Haney yelled at Ned Thompson. His face was contorted with rage, purple veins bulging on his forehead.

"Calm down, Judge," Jeb Thompson warned. "You gonna have a stroke if you keep this up."

"Shut up, Jeb! I don't need your ignorant ass telling me what to do! I'm surrounded by incompetents who can't seem to get this damn job done! What's it going to take for you people to realize the seriousness of this situation?"

"Harry, you know we're all doing the best we can," Sheriff Lucas quietly admonished, trying to calm the irate man down. He'd seen Judge Haney completely lose his temper once, and the situation had been nasty. He knew what Judge Haney was capable of.

The small room the men were meeting in was located in the back of the old courthouse, and was rank with cigarette smoke, old wood, and a host of other accumulated odors from years gone by. Sheriff Lucas had a severe sinus headache and just wanted to go home and crawl into bed. The sooner this meeting was over, the better. So he pushed his luck. "Let's just call it a night, Judge, and we can start over tomorrow."

The room became deathly quiet. Ominous. Nobody told—nobody even suggested to Judge Haney how to conduct these meetings they'd had on a monthly basis since Sam Avery had been killed and his daughter sent to prison.

Very slowly Judge Haney turned to Sheriff Lucas.

"And since when did you start running this show, William? Do you think you can do a better job than I'm doing?" If the Judge's face was red before, it was scarlet now. Sheriff Lucas hadn't calmed him down as planned, but instead had worsened the situation.

And suddenly Sheriff Lucas didn't care. He was tired of all of it. Tired of the games they'd played for all these years. As a young man, when he'd decided to become an officer for the law, he hadn't dreamed he'd become a criminal instead.

He just wanted out. At this point he didn't care if Judge Haney killed him. At least he'd have some peace. Well—maybe a moment's worth, as he passed from this life to hell, where he was sure he'd go if he continued on the path he was on now.

"The lollygagging is *over*," Judge Haney ground out. "Tomorrow I want you to find out who Mary Draper is, and if she's connected in any way with Desh Elliot, and I want you to find out where Abigail Avery is!" He said to Sheriff Lucas. "Ned and Jeb, I don't care what you have to do to make a place for the tires that are coming in next week, just make a place. Got it?"

The two cowering men nodded their agreement, so Judge

Haney focused on the three people in the back of the room who had sat quietly through the meeting. "And do you losers think it's possible you might just be able to watch the Avery place closely enough to catch who's coming and going in there whenever they damn well please?"

The three nodded their heads and chorused, "Yes!"

"Then everybody get out of here, and try not to let anyone see you all leaving together. Can you manage that?" Sarcasm dripped from his words and contempt from his demeanor. As the small group started to leave the room, he added, "And William, if you want to live to be an old man, don't *ever* correct me again."

William Lucas didn't even give Judge Harry Haney the courtesy of acknowledging him. Sheriff Lucas had made a new resolve tonight. He might not live to be an old man, but by damn he would leave this world with his head held high when he did go.

Harry Haney slammed the front door as he entered his house. It had not been a good day. All he wanted was a strong drink and to spend some relaxing time on the Internet before he turned in for the night.

He made himself a double Harvey Wallbanger and headed for his office. The first thing he noticed was the flashing light on his answering machine. His impulse was to ignore it, but then, it might be news on Abigail Avery.

He listened to the whispered message, "The end is near," three times before exploding. "Surely that little white-trash bitch doesn't think she can play with me!" he screamed at the top of his voice. He knew, without a shadow of a doubt, that the whispered message was from Abigail.

"Are you okay, Pooky?" The little-girl voice that usually turned him on just irritated him tonight. His tiny wife had heard his screaming and come to comfort him.

"Just go on back to bed, Lois, I'll be there in a little while." He tried not to let her see how upset he was. The less she knew of his business, the better, had been his motto since their marriage.

"Okay, if you're sure," she whined, and left the room.

Slugging down half his drink with one swig, Judge Haney set the glass down and picked up the phone.

When the voice on the other end answered, Judge Haney said, "The time for playing is over. I want her dead, just like her old man. If she thinks she can work me, she's just signed her death warrant."

"How do you want it done?"

"I don't care. Just try to make it look like an accident."

"How about if her lover kills her?" The malicious laugh that followed almost made even Judge Haney sick.

"You mean Desh Elliot?"

"Yeah. Then you'd have one more opponent out of the way."

"See. That's why I depend on you. You always come up with these good ideas. Go for it. Just get it done."

Chapter 14

Desh studied the maps that lay spread out on Abigail's bed in front of him. "This is one of the most amazing things I've ever seen! Whoever drew these maps of the cave system has an amazing talent! Do you think your dad did these?"

"I have no idea, but he had this money for some reason," she said, handing him the stacks of money that had been in the envelope.

Desh leafed thoughtfully through the bills. "New bills, as if someone got them from the bank for the purpose of paying a debt," he said. "But if this money is payment for drawing the maps, and your dad did the drawing, why did he still have the maps *and* the money? There should have been an exchange."

"Maybe he found this package. Or stole it," Abigail offered. "But at least I can pay you back for the clothes you bought for me. Clothes that I don't have any need for since I'm not allowed to leave this house," she finished with a tinge of resentment in her voice.

"Abigail, you forget paying me for the clothes. And you

shouldn't have spent this money on a car. In fact, you shouldn't spend any more of this money until we find out where your dad got it. If it came from a bank robbery or some other illegal means, you may have to give it back!

"What do you think these two dots are?" he asked, changing the subject.

"I think they're my house and the barn," Abigail answered.

Desh studied the drawings more closely. "You're right! So that means this huge room is on your property. It has to be, because it's so close to the two dots." Excitement tinged his voice. "Now we're getting somewhere, thanks to your determination!"

He leaned over and gave her a quick kiss. "Hmmm. That tasted good. I can't keep my mind on what I'm supposed to be doing when you're around." He pulled her close and captured her lips again. His hand moved up and gently cupped one of her breasts.

Abigail drew in a sharp breath before being filled with languid ecstasy. Nobody had ever touched her like this. Nobody had ever made her feel like this. Nobody had ever caused that heat in the center of her universe. And while she understood what it was, it still frightened her because it made her weak. Weak and vulnerable and dependent. Emotions she couldn't afford, no matter how much she wanted to explore them.

"Desh!" she gasped, pushing away from him. "Stop! We're never going to get anything done at this rate."

Desh grinned that charming Dashing Desh grin and said, "You're too afraid of your own feelings, Abigail. But I'm going to teach you to give in to them. I'm going to show you how wonderful it can be to make love with someone. I know we don't have time right now, but soon, my Abigail, soon."

His words—his promise—and the gently caressing tone of his voice stirred Abigail more than his kiss had. Her hands shook as she attempted to fold the maps.

Desh noticed and caught her hands in his own, bringing them to his lips. He kissed each finger, then turned them over and kissed each palm. "Leave the maps for now. I want to go over them some more in a few minutes. But right now I want to give you a gift I brought you from Birmingham." And still holding one of her hands, he led her downstairs.

A gift for her? What a concept! Nobody had bought her a gift since her mom died. And that had only been at Christmas time. After her mom died she hadn't gotten anything.

Before Christmas she'd sit for hours with an old Sears catalog and fantasize about the things she wished she could get. Then she'd pretend she'd gotten her favorites when the teacher asked the kids to "share" what they got for Christmas.

"Close your eyes and hold out your hands," Desh said, holding a small package behind his back.

Obediently, Abigail did what he asked, and felt a small box being placed across the palms of her outstretched hands.

"Okay, you can open them now."

Slowly, Abigail opened her eyes and looked down at an intricately designed, filigree gold rosebud on a gold chain, with matching earrings. The rosebud was just beginning to open to expose what would be a beautiful rose.

"I chose this because it reminds me of you. I think you're a beautiful rosebud, but when you finally discover the beauty that lies within yourself and realize how beautiful you really are, you're going to open into a rose that will put this one to shame. You're my beautiful rose, Abigail Avery. And this is to remind you that I've always thought so."

Abigail stared down at the stunning set. The tag on the box said 14K gold. This was an expensive gift. And yet the price of the jewelry couldn't touch the priceless gift of the words that Desh had just spoken.

Tears glistened in her eyes as she looked up at him. Was

this guy for real? Never having known love or had tender words of love spoken to her, it was so hard for her to believe them. Why did he insist that he loved her? He didn't even know her, so how could he love her? Sure, he said he'd watched her in school, but that's not like actually getting into someone's head and heart and knowing them. And she didn't know him. What was he like on a normal basis? Their brief contact since she'd been out of prison wasn't normal, in the least.

As the thoughts ran through her head, Desh took the necklace from the box, drooped it around her neck and fastened it. Following that, he fastened the earrings into her ears. Then, sliding his hands gently around her neck, he cupped her face and turned it up to him. His thumbs tenderly traced the corners of her lips.

"You'll believe me one day, Abigail. You'll believe me, and you'll feel like the most loved, most beautiful woman that ever lived. I'm not going to stop until I've convinced you of that. Then I won't stop because my love for you will never end," his husky voice assured her as he brushed her lips with a feather kiss. "Well, do you like it or not? You haven't said a word."

Abigail reached up and touched the rosebud on her neck. "Of course I love it! But, Desh—I just don't know what to say. Your gifts, your words leave my head spinning. I'm not used to this kind of treatment, and I don't think I'm very good at accepting things. Things *or* words of kindness. This is all so strange to me. And," she ended on an exasperated note, "I'm not sure you should to be doing it."

"You could just smile and say, 'Thank you.' That's all you need to say." Sensing her conflicting emotions, Desh changed the subject. "Now, go put on one of those fancy outfits you bought. I want to take Leaky Spring's visiting Realtor out to dinner."

"Do you think that's wise, after today?"

"Well, I figure they're going to come after both of us soon, so we might as well make it easy for them to find us. Besides, I'm taking you to a quaint little Mexican restaurant just outside of town, so we probably won't see anyone who'll recognize us."

"What about the maps? I thought you were going to look at those some more."

"I do want to see them. Do you mind if I take them to my room and go over them while you dress?"

He followed her to her room and collected the maps. "We need to put these and the money somewhere that can't be easily found," he said. "Because before this is over, it won't surprise me if someone breaks into this house and searches it. I'm convinced that they've been looking for this package all the time. Not the deed to your place. They don't really care about the deed because they mean to own your property one way or another. But they need these maps to find the opening to this large section of the cave system. They don't know where it is." A huge grin spread across his face. "They don't know where it is, so you and I have to find it first. This is coming together, Abigail!"

"So when are we going to look for it?" she asked.

"We're going to start our search tomorrow. We'll get up early in the morning and go to your place and see what we can find," he promised. "But in the meantime, we have tonight to think about. Just meet me downstairs when you're ready to go."

As Desh reached the door, Abigail said, "Thank you, Desh," and touched the rosebud on her neck.

Desh's heart lurched to his throat when he turned to see Abigail standing with her hand on the gift he'd given her. He started back to her but she held up her hand. "Go! I have to get dressed!" She laughed.

But seeing her with the soft look on her face was almost too much for him. He'd never seen her look—well, almost happy!

"Goodbye, Desh. Shoo!" She came over and playfully pushed him out the door and closed it.

Excitement surged through Abigail. Finally! Maybe they were about to crack this case. And when they did, she knew that most of the people on her jury would come down with the crash.

She glanced through the new clothes she'd bought with Desh's money. For some reason she felt like wearing something frilly and feminine tonight. Something far, far removed from the harsh uniforms she'd had to wear in prison.

So she chose the most feminine thing she'd bought. A periwinkle blue peasant top with a gently flowing skirt that reached almost to her ankles. The skirt had a black swirl design against its periwinkle blue background, so she chose black sandals to finish the outfit. She fluffed up her short hair and looked in the mirror. Her new gold rosebud glittered and reflected the light.

A stranger stared back at Abigail Avery. The eyes that looked back at her were soft and dreamy. The face almost appeared happy. What was happening to her? Was she turning into someone she wouldn't recognize? Someone she might not even like? All of her life she'd dreamed of being happy. Of having a "normal" life. But deep down she was afraid of seeing that dream come true because it was so foreign to anything she'd ever known.

If Desh really did love her, would she be able to accept it? Could she allow him to love her like he said he did? Would she be able to love him back?

You already do. The thought came unexpected. Unbidden. And it left Abigail weak with the knowledge of the truth. She'd loved her fantasy of Desh Elliot since she was a young girl. But that was a fantasy. The Desh Elliot that she was getting to know while living in his house was even better than her fantasy. But how could she trust this new feeling of love? Was it real?

Was he real? Or was he still just a fantasy masquerading as a wonderful man?

The skepticism that had been her constant companion for so long clouded the new knowledge that she could be in love with Desh. Clouded it, but couldn't quite smother it out this time. Hope was beginning to live in Abigail.

"We'll see," she whispered, reaching up and touching the beautiful rosebud that rested on her smooth skin.

Her heart pounded louder than normal as she headed down the stairs to join Desh.

She found him in the kitchen with the maps spread out over the table. He glanced up when she walked in and was about to comment on the maps when his head snapped back to her. The look of appreciation on his face brought a smile to Abigail's face.

"Oh my," he whispered. "You look absolutely beautiful."

"Thank you," she said. It was going to take her a while to become comfortable with his compliments, but she was trying.

"Look at this," Desh said, reaching for her shoulder. "Is this elastic around the neckline?" And he gently slid it lower on her shoulder. "Look how easy it would be to just pull this down."

"Desh Elliot! Behave yourself!" Abigail said, pushing his hand away and backing up. "If you're going to act like a sixth grader, I'll just go put on another blouse!"

"Don't even think about it," he said. His green eyes became brilliant, and a very teasing smile played havoc with those lips that had become so tempting to her.

"Desh, I'm serious!" Abigail said, as he moved closer to her.

"So am I," he answered. But he stopped just before their bodies touched. "I'm so very serious. But I'll be good for now. At least until we get back home." There was a different note in his voice as he leaned over and kissed the curve of her neck.

Abigail wanted desperately to reach out and draw him to her. Wanted to explore her newfound knowledge. Wanted to explore her feelings and desires. She realized she wanted to make love with Dashing Desh Elliot.

Not knowing what to do with emotions so new to her, Abigail turned quickly to the maps. "So? Have you come to any conclusions?"

Desh allowed her to change the subject even as adrenalin rushed through his body. He sensed something different about Abigail. A change of attitude toward him—and it was driving him crazy with desire. But he could wait. He'd waited most of his life for Abigail Avery. He could wait a little longer. Just a little longer.

"Nothing of importance. I've just been looking at them. I'll study them some more later. Let's go find some food." He folded the maps and stuck them in a cabinet.

He drove them to a quaint little Mexican restaurant outside of town. A few cars were there, but it was still early in the evening, so they were some of the first to arrive.

Abigail loved the festive atmosphere of the restaurant and that nobody seemed to notice when they walked in. Maybe they could have a relaxing, normal meal without having to worry about being seen.

"This is a first for me," she volunteered after the server had seated them and taken their drink order.

"What do you mean?" Desh asked, beginning to munch on the chips and salsa the hostess placed on the table.

"I've never been to a Mexican restaurant," she answered. "My social life has been kind of limited, as you know."

"I forget about all the things you haven't done in your life, Abigail," he said. "All the things you didn't get to do as a child, as a teenager, and as a young woman. Why, I'll bet you've never even made out in the back seat of a car, have you?" Desh was warming up to his subject. "Ah! So many things for me to teach my Abigail!"

They were seated in a booth, Desh beside her instead of across from her, making their seating arrangement very close and intimate. He slid one arm around the back of her shoulders and his other hand gently tugged at the elastic at her shoulder.

"Desh!" She scolded. "Stop that! People can see what you're doing."

"Nobody can see me. But I don't care if they do," he said, leaning down and kissing the spot on her shoulder he'd uncovered.

"Are you ready to order?" The server had an amused smile on his face as he interrupted them.

As they placed their order, Abigail was aware of a woman being seated at the table close to their booth. The woman's face was odd looking to Abigail. The features seemed surreal, and Abigail had to fight the urge to keep looking back at her.

All during the meal she found herself continuing to glance at the woman. Thankfully, she didn't seem to notice Abigail's attention. Instead, she seemed preoccupied with staring across the room at nothing at all.

After they finished their meal, Abigail decided to go to the restroom before heading back home. She had to pass a pay phone on her way to the restroom, and realized the strange woman she'd been watching all night was on the phone. The woman's back was to Abigail, so Abigail took the chance to look at her closely. She was of average height and slim, but Abigail was amazed at her small feet. They looked like a child's feet in high-heeled shoes.

As she passed by, she almost stopped in her tracks as she heard the woman's voice. It was a very deep voice—and definitely *not* a woman's.

"I'm sure it's her," the deep voice said. "She's put on weight, and her hair's a different color, but that face is the face in the picture you showed me. The reason we haven't been able to find Abigail Avery is because she got fat in prison. I can't believe some of you haven't recognized her. I guess that's why you have to call in an expert like me. You good ole' boys can't get your heads out of your asses long enough to see what's around you." The laugh that emitted from the person made the hair on the back on Abigail's neck stand up.

"So it would seem that Abigail Avery and Mary Draper are one and the same," he added with a very self-satisfied smirk.

Chapter 15

Abigail turned quickly before the person on the phone could see her, and hurried back to Desh, who had paid for the meal and was waiting for her.

"Quick, Desh, let's get in the car," she said, brushing past him and heading outside. .

"Abigail! What's wrong with you?" Desh asked after they were seated in the car.

"Drive, Desh! I'll explain in a minute. Just get us away from here!" She watched the door as she talked, to see if the mysterious man/woman was going to come out.

Desh started the car and pulled out on the street. "Now, will you tell me what's wrong with you?"

"Did you notice that woman sitting beside us in the restaurant?"

"Yeah. Kind of an odd looking character, wasn't she?"

"She's a he. That was a man, I think. At least she—he—has a man's voice. And Desh, he was sitting next to us on purpose." She explained the phone conversation she'd overheard.

"Well, it looks like we need to get ready for a showdown. This all seems to be coming together. I need to do some research on this strange little man and see if I can find out who he is. Was there anything significant that you noticed about him?"

"He had very small feet. His feet were small even for a woman. I don't know where he could have found heels that small."

"Heels?"

"Yes, his shoes."

"Hmmm." Desh seemed to be lost in thought.

"What?"

"The tracks of the person who shot at us the first night you came home were made with very small feet wearing high-heeled shoes. That's why I've suspected *The* Mrs. Harry Haney. But maybe it wasn't her."

"So what do we do now?" Abigail asked.

"Right now we try to lose the person who's been following us since we left the restaurant," he said, glancing in his rearview mirror. "No! Don't look back. I don't want them to suspect that we know they're back there." Desh turned quickly down a side street.

"How do you know they're following us?" Abigail asked.

"So far they've made every turn we have, including this one," he said. "It's hard to lose someone in a town this small, so I need to find a well lit place and see what they want. Here's the plan. When I turn at this next corner, I'll stop just long enough for you to get out of the car. The old Sears building is close enough that you can duck quickly inside before the car following us sees you. I'll find a place to stop and see what the person wants, then I'll come back for you."

"Desh—"

"There's no time to argue, Abigail—get ready!"

Desh pulled the car to the curb and Abigail quickly got out and ran to the old Sears building, which had stood on this corner for years. It was still in full operation. She watched as Desh pulled away, then turned to see if anyone followed him. To her surprise, Sheriff Lucas, driving his personal car, came around the corner and followed Desh. Sheriff Lucas?

Why was Sheriff Lucas following them at night in his own car? That didn't make any sense to Abigail. Surely that had just been coincidence!

Time crawled as Abigail stood and waited for Desh to return. But finally, she saw his car slowing down at the curb.

"Was Sheriff Lucas actually following us?" she asked as she settled in beside him.

"Yes. And he's on his way out to our place to talk with us," Desh answered.

"To talk with us?" Apprehension swept over Abigail. "Is he going to try to arrest me?" *Did he say* our *place?* she silently asked herself.

"Well, that's the odd part. It seems that Sheriff Lucas has changed sides. He wants to be our friend now."

"Do you think this is a trick? Is he just trying to get information from us?"

"That thought is uppermost in my mind. But I'll just have to feel him out. He does know you're back in town. I'm not sure he's put Mary Draper and Abigail Avery together, though. But I guess if we're going to find out what he wants, you'll have to talk with him, too."

A tiny ripple of dread crawled up Abigail's spine. What if this was just a trick to get to her? Could they send her back to jail? She didn't think she could go back to jail. Panic started to grip her as she felt pending doom.

As if sensing her fear, Desh covered her clenched hands with one of his. "Abigail, you don't have to talk with William Lucas if you don't want to. I can drop you off somewhere and come back for you, after I've talked with him."

"I just don't think I could stand going back to jail, Desh," she answered.

"Jail? They can't send you back to jail! They don't have anything on you. At this point, they don't even have some drummed up charge like they had before. You don't have to worry about going back to jail. And I don't think you have to worry about your life with Lucas. I don't think he's the dangerous one. I think he's just been a pawn in the hands of Judge Haney."

"Then let's see what he has to say," Abigail said, feeling her anxiety fade a little. After all, she'd come back to this town to get her vengeance. She couldn't do that by hiding out.

When they reached the Draper place Sheriff Lucas was already there, but he'd parked his car behind a huge shrub that grew close to the house.

"Hmmm. That's interesting," Desh mused. "I think the sheriff is trying to hide his car from anyone who might drive up and see him here. Maybe he's really going to help us."

As Desh and Abigail stepped from the car, William Lucas came from the shadows to meet them. "I hope you don't mind me parking here, Desh. I can't afford to be caught conspiring with the enemy just yet," he said.

"That's a good place for your car, William," Desh assured him as he hustled them all inside.

Once inside the living room, William Lucas turned to Abigail. "I'm William Lucas," he said, offering his hand.

Abigail glanced at Desh to see how she should react. It was obvious that Sheriff Lucas didn't recognize her.

Desh winked at her and said, "Sheriff Lucas, let me introduce you to Abigail Avery."

The surprise on the man's face was genuine. Then he burst into a big laugh.

"So that's it! This is why we didn't recognize you! The waif we sent away from Leaky Springs has turned into a beautiful woman! It is my pleasure to meet the new Abigail Avery." He took her hand in his and held it in a warm handshake.

Abigail felt a little more of the tension drain from her. Sheriff Lucas seemed to be real.

But he also seemed nervous. He kept glancing at the open windows as if expecting someone to drive up and catch him conspiring with them.

"Sit down, William," Desh said, seeming comfortable using Sheriff Lucas' first name. "Would you like something to drink? Coffee? Water? Pop?"

"I'll have some water if it's not a problem," Lucas answered, glancing at an open window before sitting in a chair that didn't require him to walk past the window.

Noticing his nervousness about the windows, Abigail proceeded to draw the drapes to close them in from any outside vision.

"Thanks," Sheriff Lucas said to Desh, when he came back with the water. "And thank you, Abigail, for closing the curtains. These woods have eyes, in case y'all didn't know."

"Oh, we've experienced a little of that," Desh said.

"How?" the sheriff asked.

"We were shot at the first night Abigail came home."

"Shot at? Where?" Concern actually showed on the sheriff's face.

"We were in her kitchen and someone shot at us with a rifle."

"So that's why Harry called that little weasel in on this action," Sheriff Lucas mused.

"Who?" Desh asked. "What weasel?"

"Tiny Roper. He's a marksman from Dallas that Harry's wife met before they were married."

"I thought it might be *The* Mrs. Harry Haney, herself," Desh said. "I found a lot of small high-heeled shoe prints in the spot where the shooter stood."

"Well, that wouldn't be Lois Haney," William Lucas

chuckled. "She has huge feet. That's the one spot on her body she can't fix with plastic surgery. But if she could, she'd have her feet removed and smaller ones put on, she hates them so much."

"Does this Tiny dude like to dress as a woman?" Desh asked. "We saw someone in the restaurant tonight who appeared to be an incredibly strange looking woman, then Abigail heard this person on the phone and she said *it* had a very deep man's voice."

"That's Tiny," William confirmed. "He *is* a very strange person. He's actually married and has two kids, but he dresses like a woman to conceal his identity when he's on a job."

"William, before we get too deep into our conversation with you, I have to ask you how serious you are about helping us. Why now? Why the change of heart?" Desh asked.

"You have every right to be suspicious," Sheriff Lucas answered. "Ten years ago when I was just starting out in my new job as Sheriff over Leaky Springs, I was excited about being a sheriff. I was ready to take on the world and make a difference in the crime scene. Of course, I knew the small town of Leaky Springs didn't have much crime, but when Harry Haney contacted me and offered me the job I jumped at the chance. I was just out of the Academy when Harry called and offered the job to me. Old Sheriff Hargrove had just died. Harry said he had to appoint a new sheriff and nobody in Leaky Springs wanted the job. I should have known that sounded suspicious, but I was too young and naive. And that's what he was looking for. Someone he could train to do his dirty work. Someone he could control.

"When your dad was killed, Abigail, I wasn't allowed to investigate the murder. I was told that you were the one who did it. That it was a cut-and-dried case. I never saw the crime scene. I did walk in on Harry putting the shotgun that killed your father into the crematory with your dad's body."

Noticing Abigail's puzzled look, he stopped.

"I didn't realize my dad was cremated," she said.

"Harry said because he was so poor the county had to bury him, that was the least expensive way," the sheriff explained kindly. "He said one thing that I didn't pay a lot of attention to at the time, but recently, it has come to my mind several times. When I walked in on him tossing the shotgun in with your father, he kind of shrugged and told me that if I ever wanted to destroy evidence, fire was the safest way. But like I said, I didn't think much about that, so when you were convicted and sent to prison, I truly believed you were guilty. But recently I've been hearing little snippets of things that have led me to believe differently. And I've been trying to remember and go back over all the reasons Harry gave me for not investigating the murder more than we did. At the time they seemed reasonable, but now those reasons seem very shallow."

"What reasons did he give you?" Desh asked.

"Well—" William hesitated, looking embarrassedly at Abigail.

"Go ahead, Sheriff Lucas, there's not much that can surprise me, now," Abigail assured him.

"His main reason that he suspected you killed your dad was because y'all, and I quote him, 'were poor white trash and your dad was probably sexually molesting you, so you just killed him.'"

Both men looked questioningly at Abigail when a harsh laugh escaped her throat. But she just shook her head, indicating she didn't want to discuss the thought that brought such a bitter response from her. Not now. But she would surely discuss it later.

So William continued, "Harry has kept me pretty much in the dark about his affairs until recently. I don't think he wanted me to know too much in case there was some kind of investigation. He wanted 'his' sheriff to look clean. But last night I realized just how much I was under his command. And I didn't like what I saw when I looked in the mirror." He stopped talking long enough to take a big swig of water. "So I decided to take my life back while I still have enough time to do a little good in this world before it's too late."

"Meaning?" Desh questioned.

"Meaning now I'm on your side. I'm going to do whatever it takes to stop what's about to happen."

"Are the judge and his followers going to try and send Abigail back to prison?" Desh asked.

"No. I don't think they'll try that again. It might look too suspicious."

"Are they going to try to kill me?" Abigail asked.

"I don't think they'll go that far—" William hesitated.

"But?" Abigail and Desh asked together.

"But they do intend to have your property, one way or the other. Since having you in jail didn't convince you to sell to them, I don't think they'll go that route again. But Abigail, if you don't sell to them, I'm not sure they won't try to kill you. If you're dead, with no surviving heirs, the property will go to the state. Then they'll have what they want. I don't mean to frighten you, but I do believe this situation has become extremely serious. That's why I want to help."

In fact, Sheriff William Lucas knew deep in his heart that they would kill Abigail Avery if they needed to. He knew, now, that he'd seen that happen on several occasions. Abigail's dad was just one of them. Other than her dad's, the deaths always looked like accidents, but in retrospect, he knew better. For instance, someone like Roy Thompson, who had spent his life roaming the hills around here, didn't accidentally fall off of one of them and kill himself. Roy had probably gotten tired of kowtowing to Judge Haney—and lost his life for it.

"Do you have any suggestions where we should go from here?" Desh asked. "Do you know anything about their plans?

Why is Abigail's property so valuable to them?"

"Judge Haney is illegally dumping tires in the caves around here. The one he's using behind the Thompsons' gas station is almost running over, so they're becoming desperate for the caverns that run under Abigail's property."

"So you know about that?" Desh asked.

"Most everyone knows the caverns are there, but nobody seems to know how to get to them. Judge Haney seems to know that the opening is on Abigail's property, but not where it is. But there's something else he's looking for. He keeps telling his goons to keep searching for "the information" in Abigail's house. I tried to find out what he's talking about, but he clams up when I ask."

"It's a map of the caverns," Desh volunteered.

"A map?"

"Yes, someone has drawn an elaborate map of the cavern system that runs this entire area."

"Do you have it here?" William asked.

"We know where it is," Desh hedged.

"So that's it," William mused. "Well, my suggestion is that you don't tell anyone else you know about that, or they'll come after you, Desh. They'll swarm this house if they have any suspicion that you know about the map. Harry seems to be getting desperate to find it."

"This illegal dumping that you referred to—can we get the EPA in on this and stop the good judge in his tracks?" Desh asked. He had to find out if the sheriff knew of the EPA's investigation.

"As crooked as Judge Haney is, he's probably paying off someone in the EPA office," William answered.

Desh decided not to mention that he'd been working with the EPA on this for some time. "We've got to find a way to bring him down, William. He's too dirty to keep breathing the same air as the decent folks in Leaky Springs."

"Trust me, there's a way to bring him down," Abigail interjected. "And it has nothing to do with dumping tires in a few caves."

Chapter 16

As both men's heads swiveled to look at Abigail at the same time, the shrill ringing of the phone stopped any comment they may have had.

Desh glanced at the caller ID and said, "Excuse me, I need to take this. It's the hospital."

Abigail watched Desh's face as he listened to the voice on the phone and knew the news wasn't good.

"Dad's gone," Desh said, lowering the phone to the base. "He had a massive heart attack while they were running tests on him. There was nothing they could do to save him." He raked his hands through his hair as he fought his emotions. "If you'll excuse me?" Before either could answer, he'd left the room.

"I really hate to hear that," Sheriff Lucas said, looking at Abigail. "His dad was a fine man."

"I never really got to know him," Abigail said. "But I'm sure he was a good man. He sure raised a good son."

"Abigail, I don't mean to be nosy, but what did you mean

about bringing Judge Haney down?"

"I'm not at liberty to tell you right now. But I know things that the public won't take sitting down."

"That sounds pretty ominous. I can't imagine anything that could be bad enough to stop Judge Harry Haney."

"Trust me, Sheriff Lucas, there's nobody who can't be taken down."

"Wow. The little Abigail Avery I remember sure has changed."

"That's what ten years of prison will do to a person, William." Abigail didn't quite trust the sheriff. Even though he seemed sincere about his new mission to help them, still, she'd learned that you can't trust everybody.

"Well, I guess I'll go. I'll call Desh tomorrow and give him my condolences."

Three days had passed since the news of Ted Elliot's death. His funeral services would begin in an hour.

"I don't like leaving you here alone," Desh said, coming down the staircase. "But you'll be safer here than at the funeral. Too many people know who you are by now."

Abigail was aware of the quickening of her heartbeat as she looked at Desh. He was stunningly sexy in his black suit, white shirt, and silver tie. His thick blond hair was more styled than she'd ever seen it. She liked it better when he'd just tousled it by running a hand through it, as was his habit.

She'd tried to find words to comfort him during the past three days, but she felt as if she'd failed miserably. Other than her mother, she'd never lost anyone she loved, so she didn't know the right words to say. Didn't even know how it felt.

As if sensing her need to comfort him, Desh walked to her and pulled her close. She wrapped her arms around him and held him tightly as he buried his face in her neck. Brief seconds passed before he pulled away, kissed her gently on the lips, and left.

Abigail sat on the couch and relived the moment. For some reason his actions had touched her more than anything he'd ever done. He'd drawn comfort from her. Just for a brief moment, he'd allowed *her* to be the strong one.

At that moment, Abigail understood what a relationship was supposed to be like. Not one person always being strong for the other, but each being able to lean on the other when they needed comfort.

She had so much to learn about life. Having never been around a couple who had a loving relationship, she had no idea what to expect. What to work toward. But she could learn. Desh could teach her. His parents apparently had a wonderful marriage.

Desh could teach her? Abigail came to attention on the couch. Where had that come from? How long had she entertained the idea of actually taking Desh Elliot up on his constant proposals? She was sure he was teasing—most of the time, anyway. Wasn't he?

"Make a move and I'll blow your brains out." The cold voice matched the metal that had been gently laid against the flesh on her neck.

Abigail recognized the voice of the man/woman at the restaurant.

"Don't look around. Don't even breathe deeply. Just get off the couch and walk out the back door. There's a car parked in the back yard. Get in it and close the door."

Abigail's mind was quickly working on a way to get out of the situation.

"And if you don't hurry up, you'll be found here in a puddle of blood just like your old man was."

Abigail didn't doubt for a moment that the threat would be carried out if she made the wrong move. She quickly got off the couch and headed for the back door, as instructed. A long black Cadillac was parked in the back yard. Tinted windows hid the inside of the car. Nobody could be seen from inside.

How had that car gotten back here without her hearing it? Had she been so lost in her thoughts about Desh that she'd tuned out everything around her?

She opened the back door of the car and sat down. A black panel separated the back seat from the front, so she couldn't see who got in and started the car. The doors had automatically locked when they closed, and there were no handles to open them from the inside of the back seat.

How many people have ridden to their deaths in this car? she suddenly wondered. *Am I riding to mine?* She gulped down the cold fear that tried to rise in her throat.

Where was this weirdo taking her? She tried in vain to see through the windows, but was only greeted by a black reflection of her own face. She glanced frantically around the car in hopes of finding a way to open the doors, but there was no way out.

Could she kick a window out? And if she succeeded, could she jump from the car before he/she shot her? Probably not.

Taking deep, calming breaths, Abigail managed to quiet herself down a little. She had to keep her head so she could take advantage of any chance of escape, should it arise.

After what seemed like hours but was probably more like minutes, she felt the car slowing to a stop. The back door was snatched open and a huge hand reached in and roughly pulled her from the car.

"Damn! Are you sure this is the right woman? I don't remember Abigail Avery being this big!"

"Shut up, dimwit! Just lead her." A flashlight was turned on to lead the way through a long corridor.

Abigail soon realized they were in what looked like the basement of an old building. She'd thought at first they were in a cave, because of the total darkness.

She smelled the stale scent of old wood, old paper and old

books. Kind of like the way the courthouse used to smell. Is that where they'd brought her? To the very chambers of Judge Harry Haney?

They led her up a long flight of stairs and opened a door to another completely dark room. Before she had time to wonder what was in the room, a heavy hand slapped her behind the head, knocking her to the floor. "That should keep her quiet for awhile," she heard Dimwit say, just before total blackness engulfed her.

Damp and chilled, Abigail slowly regained consciousness. How
long had she been out? Her head had hit something just before she'd hit the floor. She felt her head to see if she was bleeding. Her hand rested on a lump that fit into her palm, but no blood seemed apparent.

What had she hit? She moved her hands slowly around to try and feel the object. She found what seemed to be the leg of a chair or table. She pulled on it, but it didn't move, so it must be a table. Seemingly a very sturdy table, she decided as she used the leg to help pull herself to a sitting position.

As she shuffled around to sit up, she heard scurrying sounds in the far corners. Mice? Even worse, rats?

Feeling a sudden urgency to get off the floor, she used the leg of the table to pull herself up. Groping around in the blackness, she discovered that the table was fairly large and sturdy enough that she felt comfortable sitting on it.

Her head throbbed and she felt queasy. She probably had a concussion. Exhausted from her ordeal, she felt along the table and found, to her delight, that it was big enough for her to lie down on. She curled into the fetal position and placed her head on her arm. She started drifting back to sleep, wondering if that was a good idea if she had a concussion, but too tired to fight it.

"If you ever need a place to hide from him, just come out

here." Her mom's voice came to her out of the darkness.

It had been one of those really bad times when her dad had been on a week's drunk and had hit her mom on a couple of occasions during the week. Her mom had led her to the barn and to the very back corner. A corner where little sunlight ever seemed to shine. There, she'd hauled a bale of hay away from a trap door and led them down into a cave.

It all came back to Abigail now. Once inside the cave, her mom had lit a lantern to expose a room with a table and chair. The table had been large enough for them to spend the night on. Curling up on this table in the pitch dark had brought the memory back to Abigail. And maybe the lick on the head had helped, she mused, again touching the tender lump.

Why had she blocked that memory? Maybe that's why she always felt safe in the barn, but just couldn't remember why.

Why would she have blocked it? Closing her eyes, she willed herself to remember more. The next morning her mother had led her back to the house, hoping her dad would have slept off his drunken meanness.

But once they got to the house, he'd started in on her mom again. "Tucked your tail and ran back to Mama and Daddy again, didn't you? That's what you always do when you can't stand the heat of being married to a real man! You always run back home!" By now he was yelling, and Abigail had run to her room to try and drown out their voices.

When things had quieted down, Abigail had ventured timidly from her room. She'd asked where her mom was and that was when her dad said her mom had fallen and hurt herself. Said that help was on the way. But when the ambulance got there, it was too late. Her mom was dead.

Suddenly Abigail knew why she'd blocked that night with her mom. It had been the last night they'd spent together. And suddenly she knew with clarity that her dad had killed her mom. Maybe not deliberately. Maybe they'd been in a shoving match, but purposefully or accidentally, her dad had been the cause of her mom's death.

And little Abigail Avery couldn't take the trauma. She'd blocked the night from her memory.

She was sitting up on the table, now. All tiredness had left her body, to be replaced by surging adrenalin. So was the cave where her mom had taken her "the opening" that everyone was looking for?

Desperate to get out of her present situation, Abigail pierced the darkness with her eyes. Surely if she was in a building in town, there'd be light coming in through a crack somewhere.

Mentally retracing her steps as she was brought into the room, she tried to imagine where the door was. If she had fallen straight, then it shouldn't be too hard to walk straight back to it.

She slid off the table. Afraid she wouldn't be able to find her way back to it if she didn't find the door, she reluctantly let go of the security of the sturdy table and took slow steps forward. Hands outstretched to keep from running head on into a wall, she moved slowly, stopping every few steps to try and keep her bearing.

Just before giving up, her hand touched something solid. Sliding both hands along the cool wood, she searched for the doorknob. Jubilation engulfed her as her hand finally closed around the coveted object. She knew the door would be locked, but she had to try it anyway. Amazement filled her when she felt the latch in the door giving way as she turned it.

They hadn't locked the door! Had they been so sure she would never find her way to it in the dark? Had they thought she'd be too afraid to try? Or did they want her to get out?

Expecting to see someone sitting guard outside, waiting to shoot her, she cautiously eased the door open. Instead, she was greeted with more darkness.

She remembered the flashlight lighting the way up a stairway to this door. But did the stairway go on up? In her befuddled memory, she wanted to think that the stairs led higher to another floor. Standing in the dark, trying to remember, Abigail became aware of a thin strip of light high above her.

Was that a door to another room? Or did it lead outside?

Chapter 17

Feeling her way through the darkness, Abigail found the staircase and slowly made her way up the steps. Occasionally one would squeak and she'd stop and wait a few moments before continuing.

Step by careful step, she moved toward the thin ray of light coming from under what she assumed now was a door. At any moment, she expected her assailants to burst through the door and catch her on the stairs.

Finally Abigail sensed that she was on a solid floor. Still she cautiously inched her feet along, making sure not to trip over another step or some object on the floor.

As she inched along she realized she was probably in a hallway, and the light she saw was coming from a door to her right, so she made her way toward it.

When she reached the door she stopped and listened for several seconds to see if there was any movement or voices on the other side. Where was the light coming from? Was it a light that was left on for safety? Or was someone still in the building?

And what building was she in?

A sense of deja vu kept telling her she was in the old courthouse. Memories from her childhood, of being surrounded by the same clawing scents that had engulfed her when her captors led her into this building, kept crowding into her mind.

But she hadn't blocked *those* memories. They would always be with her. They had kept her strong during her prison sentence. They'd kept her determined to come home and get revenge on the man who'd tainted her childhood innocence and who had stolen ten years of her life. Whether Judge Haney had killed her father was irrelevant to her. She had enough hatred for him on the other things he'd done to last a lifetime. Killing her father had actually been a favor to her.

Strengthened by angry memories and renewed determination, Abigail carefully found the doorknob and quietly turned it. Again, surprisingly, it opened to her touch.

Holding her breath, she eased the door open and found herself surrounded by a strong odor that flooded her with the same memories that had been clawing at her mind all night. But this time the odor was so overpowering she had to clamp her hands over her mouth to keep from screaming.

Breathe. Calm down. Slowly, slowly she brought her emotions under control and glanced around her. She knew where she was before confirming it by the dim light. She stood in Judge Harry Haney's office closet, where his robes hung. Where he hung his own coat or jacket when he put his robes on. The same closet where he had—

NO! She couldn't think about that right now. She had to concentrate on getting out of this building. Was he still here? She knew from the past where his desk would sit. Where he would be if he was still in his office.

Stealthily, almost without breathing, Abigail made her way through the stale, cigarette-scented robes and miscellaneous clothes to the end of the long closet. The door of the closet stood slightly ajar, allowing her to peek through.

Her greatest fear was realized. Judge Haney sat at his desk, his back toward her, gazing at a computer screen. It took Abigail a moment to realize what he was looking at.

Heat engulfed her. Bile, strong and bitter, rose in her throat, threatening to spew from her mouth.

She had to get out of here! If she stayed one more moment she'd kill the son-of-a-bitch with her bare hands! Then she *would* go back to prison.

Without thinking of anything except escaping as quietly as possible, Abigail headed back the way she'd come. One thought was on her mind. Get as far away from Judge Haney as possible, for now.

If the other doors were left unlocked, maybe the outside door her captors had brought her in through was still unlocked. Why hadn't she thought of that before? When she'd come out of the room where they'd put her, she'd seen the light, and went toward it. She should have gone back down the way they brought her up, she chided herself.

But then you wouldn't have the evidence you need, a small voice of reason interjected.

Abigail stopped in her quick descent of the staircase. *She had him!* Jubilation washed away the horror that had driven her from the scene above. She had him! What she'd just witnessed was all the proof she needed to take this cheap, low-life scum of a wannabe human being down.

Using the wall as a guide, she made her way to the bottom of the staircase and, after several false attempts, found the door. It was locked.

Her first impulse was to bang on the door and scream for help, but reason stepped in and warned her not to do that. So instead, she sank to the bottom stair step and buried her face in her hands.

Think! She had to think of a way out of here. Desh would probably be worried to death about her by now. Would he be looking for her? The thought brought renewed hope to Abigail. Renewed determination.

Surely when daylight came she'd be able to find a way out. She'd just have to sit here and wait until it got light enough to see.

She had no way of telling how long she'd sat in the one spot, but her thoughts were rampant with plans for the big bad judge. Briefly, she wondered why Judge Haney's closet opened into a hallway. And why the door was unlocked. Obviously, the hallway was a little-used one that led outside to the back alley. And there was her answer! It was his quick escape if he needed it. The fact that it was unlocked was probably a big mistake.

One of the first things she had to do was talk with Mabelle Henley. Mabelle had alluded to a real hatred she had for Judge Haney. Had he done to her what he did to Abigail? If so, how many other women in this town could tell the same story?

As she formed her plan of attack, the world outside the door began to lighten up. Abigail noticed the light under the door and stood to explore it more closely. She was about to try the doorknob again when she heard voices outside. Should she call out? Before she could make a decision, she heard a key in the lock and the door was pushed open, wedging her behind it.

The two who'd brought her there headed up the stairs, never looking back. They'd pushed the door closed, but hadn't taken time to lock it.

Instantly Abigail opened the door and stepped outside. Glancing around to make sure nobody was watching, she realized she was in the alley that ran behind Front Street.

She had to disappear quickly. But where? It was too early for the stores to be open. But maybe she could catch someone who had come in to put up stock. She dodged between the jewelry store and the Sears building.

Footsteps pounded behind her. Not looking around, she stepped onto Front Street, hoping against hope that someone would be stirring. She didn't believe the two men would grab her if there were witnesses. Especially if she screamed like bloody hell!

Just as she was giving up hope she saw Mr. Crabtree get out of his car and head for the Sears building. Mr. Crabtree had been the bookkeeper for Sears as long as she could remember.

She hurried toward him. "Good morning, Mr. Crabtree," she called.

Startled, he looked around. "Yes? May I help you?"

"Mr. Crabtree, please open the door and let us in. I'll explain when we're inside. I'm being chased by two men who have kept me hostage all night. Please hurry!"

Sensing her urgency, the old man reluctantly unlocked the door to the building and they stepped inside the foyer. But before unlocking the other door, he turned to her. "Now, young lady, I may be old, but I'm not stupid. Are you trying to rob me? Is this a trick to get inside the store?"

Anxiously Abigail glanced outside, but nobody was in view. "Mr. Crabtree, I'm Abigail Avery. I don't know if you remember me or not."

"Of course I remember you. You were sent to prison for killing your father. Not that anyone with any brain would believe that story," he added, unlocking the main door to the building. "Come with me, child. We'll go up to my office. Nobody can see us from there if they happen to look inside the building."

For the first time in many hours Abigail drew in a deep breath of relief, as the old man led her up a flight of stairs to the second floor offices.

She had to call Desh and let him know she was okay. Asking permission to use Mr. Crabtree's phone, Abigail was disappointed when she got Desh's answering machine. Where was he this early in the morning? The clock on the wall verified that it was only 6:30 A.M. Was he out looking for her?

She left him a message saying she was okay, but couldn't come home yet, and gave him a brief explanation.

"Would you like some coffee?" Mr. Crabtree asked as she hung up the phone.

"That would be wonderful," Abigail answered. "Do you have a phone book? I need to make another call."

After handing her the book, the old man went back to busily making his morning pot of coffee in a dingy pot that sat on the far side of his desk. He went to his private restroom and got water to go in the pot.

Abigail watched him putter around as she waited for Mabelle Henley to answer her home phone. Surely Mabelle wasn't at the Salon yet. Finally, just as Abigail was about to hang up, Mabelle's breathless voice answered, "Yes?"

"Mabelle, it's Abigail."

"Abigail? What are you doing calling me this early? I was in the shower and almost didn't hear the phone ringing."

"I hate to ask you this, but could you come over to the Sears building and pick me up?"

"What? Abigail, what's going on? What are you doing at the Sears building? They don't even open until ten o'clock!"

"Hang on," Abigail said into the phone, turning to see why Mr. Crabtree was gently tapping her on the shoulder.

"That's not a good idea, Abigail. I just saw two suspicious men watching this building from across the street. They know that I'm the only one in any of the stores yet, and they may think I've let you in."

Mabelle could hear his conversation from her end of the line and became more curious.

"Abigail? What does he mean two men are watching the store?"

"Two of Judge Haney's goons kidnapped me yesterday from Desh's and they locked me up in the courthouse. But I managed to escape this morning and they're looking for me."

"Do you want me to get Desh?"

"I just called him and he didn't answer his phone."

"Hang on," Abigail said, turning again to Mr. Crabtree, who was looking out the window to the street below. His grunt had gotten her attention.

"They're heading this way," he said. "I'll get rid of them." And he headed for the door, but turned and added, "I'm not going to unlock the door for them, but if they're stupid enough to try to break in, you go through that door, right there. That's the fire escape that leads downstairs to the back alley."

"Thanks, Mr. Crabtree," Abigail called to his stooped, departing back.

"Abigail, I heard what he said. Why don't you make a break for it while he's talking with them? Go out the back door, like he said, and run over to my Salon. Go to the back door of the Salon, and look under the back limb of the fake Ficus tree. I have a key taped to the limb just in case I lock myself out. I'll get there as soon as I get dressed."

Abigail felt horrible about running out on Mr. Crabtree, but Mabelle's plan seemed logical, so she hung up the phone and headed for the stairs.

As her shaking hand inserted the key into the lock of Mabelle's salon, Abigail heard a distinct sound in the distance. A gunshot. Had they killed Mr. Crabtree? Horror engulfed her as she closed the door and locked it. Had that nice old man lost his life because of her?

Sickened at the thought, she made her way to the front of the Salon where she could watch from the window. She heard sirens and saw Sheriff's Lucas' car speed down the street toward the Sears building. She waited, practically holding her breath, to see if an ambulance or fire truck followed. Minutes passed and nothing happened.

"It's a good thing you left when you did," Mabelle said behind her.

Abigail jumped so violently she almost knocked some cosmetics off the table she'd been standing beside.

"I'm sorry, Abigail, I thought you heard me come in the back door."

"No, I guess I was too intense waiting to see if an ambulance came by. I think they shot Mr. Crabtree."

"They shot the lock off the door when he refused to let them in. He's okay," Mabelle assured her.

"How do you know that?"

"I have a police scanner at the house. I heard Mr. Crabtree call Sheriff Lucas and tell him what they'd done and that they were searching the building."

"I'm sure glad you had the idea of me coming over here. But I don't want to put you in danger, Mabelle."

"Not to worry. They don't know I'm here. I walked from home. I just live a couple of blocks from here. I made sure nobody saw me."

"Mabelle, you indicated when I first came here that you really hate Judge Haney. I need to know why."

Weary from being up all night, Desh checked in Abigail's room one more time to see if maybe she'd made it home while he was gone. But her bed was still unmade.

Almost sick with worry, now, he made his way back down the stairs. He would call William Lucas to see if he knew anything.

When he'd gotten home from his dad's funeral and found Abigail gone, he'd assumed she'd decided to do some exploring. Although that didn't make any sense, since he felt sure she understood the danger she was in. Wherever she'd gone, she'd gone on foot because her car was still out front.

He'd waited a few hours, but when it started to get dark, he'd gotten really worried and started looking for her. Had she gone to her house? Had she taken a chance and walked down the road? Knowing Abigail, like he was just beginning to know her, he wouldn't put it past her. She knew his dad had been a fairly prominent figure in the community in his day, so she may have assumed that most folks would be at his funeral.

But crooks didn't attend prominent figures' funerals. At least, not the kind of crooks who had become involved with her case.

As Desh passed the living room, he saw the blinking light on his answering machine. Hurrying to it, he listened in stunned amazement to Abigail's message.

"Hi Desh, it's Abigail. I'm okay, but I wanted to let you know that a couple of Judge Haney's goons kidnapped me yesterday and locked me up in the courthouse. I managed to escape, but I can't tell you where I am and I can't come home right now because that's probably the first place they'll come looking for me. Be careful, Desh, and don't worry about me. I'll be okay. I'll be back as soon as I think it's safe."

Cold anger flooded him. He'd hoped he could hold this off until he got a little more condemning information against the judge, but he had to act now.

The EPA might not find enough to jail Judge Harry Haney right now, but they could keep the dirty bastard busy for a few days until he could get to the bottom of the rest of this mystery. He picked up the phone and made a call.

Chapter 18

Desh's house was dark as Mabelle's car approached it without the use of headlights. Thankfully the moon was bright tonight, which had allowed her to turn the lights off before entering the lane that led to the house.

"You be careful, Mabelle," Abigail said before getting out of the car. "And thank you so much for your help. We've got the dirty bastard, now. With our testimonies and the other proof you're getting, Judge Harry Haney will spend more than ten years behind bars. If this world is lucky, he'll never see daylight again!"

"I'm so glad you came back, Abigail. I've lived my life in fear and dread that he could somehow use the information he has on me. That's his mode of operation, as we know. Blackmail. For the first time in years I'm not afraid, thanks to you."

Abigail hurried to the house while Mabelle drove back down the lane. She didn't have a key, and was about to knock on the door when it was snatched quickly open.

"Abigail! Where have you been?" Desh pulled her inside

and closed the door.

"With Mabelle," she managed to get out before being smothered in his arms.

"I've been worried sick about you ever since I got your message," he said, holding her close.

There were no lights on anywhere in the house, but moonlight filtered in through the windows, casting a dim glow throughout the living room.

"Why aren't your drapes pulled, Desh? Anyone could look inside."

"I've been sitting here looking out most of the night. I'd just dozed off when I heard you come up on the porch."

"Did they come looking for me?"

"Not yet. That's what I've been waiting for. I thought they might try to break in at night. I wanted to catch them if they did."

He still held her close to him. "Oh, Abigail, I've been so worried about you. When I got your message I wanted to kill everyone connected to Judge Haney. I had visions of saving him for last!"

"We really have to talk, Desh, but after the night I had last night and the day I've had today, I wonder if I might be able to get a nap first? I don't want to take time to sleep, but I feel like I may drop on my feet if I don't. I know it's not fair to ask you to wait to hear about my ordeal, but there's way more than I can tell in just a few minutes."

"I can wait. Just knowing you're okay is all I need right now. But let's go down in the cave. I just can't take the chance of them finding you again. Not tonight. There'll be some distractions for them tomorrow, but we have to make it until then."

"What do you mean?"

"I'll explain after you've rested."

Desh grabbed a blanket and they headed for the basement.

Very carefully, he pulled a rug over the trapdoor to the cave as he lowered it, just in case anyone made it to the basement looking for them.

He found some soft, sandy silt where they could sit. They settled back against the wall, and Desh wrapped the blanket around them to ward off the damp coolness of the cave. Abigail quickly nestled her head on his shoulder, feeling as if she had come home, and was soon fast asleep. She was safe, at last.

Hearing her soft, rhythmic breathing, Desh knew she was asleep. He nestled his cheek on the top of her head and rested. He wouldn't get any sleep tonight, but being this close to Abigail was better than sleep. Knowing she was safe was more rewarding than anything he could think of right now.

This would soon be over. He wasn't sure how, but he was sure it would be over. It had to be. He had to find a way to bring closure to her past ten years of hell. Actually, her hell had been going on much longer than ten years.

He desperately wanted to show her how much he loved her. He knew he could make her happy if she'd let him. But was she ready to let him show her? He thought she trusted him now, but did she love him yet?

He'd have to work on that later. Right now he had other things to take care of. In the morning the EPA would swarm Thompson's Tire Shop and Judge Harry Haney's office. Desh broke into a big grin just imagining the look on Harry Haney's face when he was put under arrest for illegally dumping tires. The *Honorable* Judge Harry Haney would be splashed across the front pages of all the papers in this entire area.

Desh wouldn't be there to witness it, but he'd made sure that several of the regional papers and TV stations had received "anonymous" calls about what was going down. Everyone within a hundred miles would know.

But Desh was afraid that wouldn't be enough to put the judge behind prison bars. When the EPA had contacted him about helping them, their main goal was to find who was running the illegal business and put a stop to it. Sure, they'd slap a fine on him, but since it would be a first-time offense, that's probably all that would happen. They'd probably make him clean up the tires, which would take some time and a lot of money out of the Judge's bank account. But that still wasn't enough.

But there was that other "thing" that he'd heard bits and pieces of. The mystery that kept niggling at his subconscious. Vague mentionings of Judge Haney's blackmailing people in Leaky Springs and other areas. This was something Desh couldn't get a grip on. When he'd casually ask about it, people would clam up and almost run away from him. There was something going on other than the dumping. Desh knew it. He just couldn't pinpoint it—yet.

Abigail shifted positions and her lips came dangerously close to his. What would she do if he kissed her awake? Temptation flooded through him, but he knew how tired she was. He would let her sleep. Temptations would be satisfied soon enough, he promised himself, briefly placing a feather kiss on her slightly parted lips.

Disturbed, Abigail changed her position again, taking away some of the temptation. Desh placed his cheek back on the top of her head and dozed off.

The distant sound of heavy trucks woke Desh first. Slowly, Abigail came awake.

"This is perfect timing!" Desh said.

"What do you mean?" Abigail was fully awake now.

"I called the EPA on Judge Harry Haney," Desh said. "They'll arrive tomorrow—or is it today by now? I sent them to the Thompsons' garage and to Harry Haney's home. Hopefully, they'll catch the trucks in action."

"I think I know where the other cave opening is," Abigail said.

"What?"

"Last night, when I was being held in the courthouse, I remembered something that I hadn't thought about since the night my mom died."

"Wait," Desh said, as the trucks became too loud for him to hear her. After they'd faded into the distance, he asked her to continue.

She related her memory of the night her mom died. Or was killed.

As she finished, she said, "So I think the opening they're looking for is in a corner of my barn. But that wouldn't be big enough for trucks to pass though."

"Unless that's just part of the opening," Desh said.

"Maybe if we hurry, we can find where they are," Abigail said.

They hurried through the cave and came out into the woods behind the barn. Making sure nobody was around to see them, they quickly made their way into the old building.

Once inside, Abigail had to stop and try to remember which corner her mom had gone to the night they were there. She tried to keep her mind off of the stall where Betsy's remains lay.

Common sense told her it might be the corner closest to the cave where they just were, so she headed for that corner. Sure enough, an old mound of hay was in the corner. It looked as if it had once been a bale, but the strings had long since given away to let the hay slide to a heap.

"I think it's here," she whispered to Desh.

Together they started to dig into the pile of hay, and before long they found a door in the floor. Desh lifted the door and shined his flashlight into the hole to reveal steps leading downward. He went in first, brushing away cobwebs and making sure no spiders were hanging around. Once his feet touched the floor, he shined the light back up for Abigail to follow him.

When her feet were on solid ground, Desh flashed the light around a room that was about a 15-foot circle. A long table sat in the middle of the room. An old oil lamp rested on the table beside what looked like a metal box.

"What's that?" Abigail asked. Immediately, she sensed this was something that belonged to her mom.

"Abigail, we can explore that later, but if we're going to try to see where those vehicles went, we need to try to find a way out of this room, if there is one. Right now, it looks like this may be just one small room." He busily ran the light over the walls as he talked.

"Wait!" Abigail grabbed his arm and flashed the beam of light on a crevice she'd noticed. As they got closer they realized it was a very large opening instead of a crevice. The shadows had disguised the opening, making it appear small.

They found themselves in a huge cavern. As Desh traveled around the cave with the light, they were amazed to see beautiful stalactites and stalagmites in every direction. In the distance a waterfall cascaded down a tall wall to form a large pool. The light glistened on the water.

"This is beautiful, Desh! It's a shame someone like Judge Haney would actually destroy this kind of beauty."

"There's no telling how much he's already destroyed. People like him don't care about anything except their own greed."

"That's a fact. If they don't care about destroying human life, they sure don't care about nature." Bitterness sounded in Abigail's voice.

"But we need to go on. We can explore this later, too."

As Desh trudged deeper into the gaping hole, they became aware of distant machinery. They followed the sounds, drawing closer and closer to the mystery that had eluded them until now.

Suddenly they were peering down about twenty feet into another very large room of the cave. But this room had no resemblance to the magical world they'd just come through. The room below them was marred with ugliness.

Row after row of stacks of tires lined the walls of the cave, until there was barely enough room for trucks to be manipulated through the teetering piles. Just enough room was left to allow two big dump trucks to deposit their loads and drive in a circle to go back out the way they'd come in. From the lights of the vehicles, several workers could be seen stacking the tires up in yet another row.

As if on cue the engines of the trucks were silenced, and a voice shattered the brief quiet. "I'm telling you, two more hauls is the most that can be put in here. That's all!" An irate Ned Thompson was speaking.

"What about the pit?" The voice came from the shadows, but Abigail recognized it instantly. Judge Harry Haney.

"We can try burnin' them in the hole, but I don't believe they'll burn fast enough to keep up with the amount of tires that's being brought in here," Ned answered. "Even if we keep it burning round the clock it just won't do the job."

Before the conversation could go any further, two official-looking black Cadillacs pulled in behind the dump trucks. Four men wearing suits got out of each car.

"Caught with the goods!" Desh whispered.

"Who're you? And what the hell you doin' in here?" Jeb Thompson bellowed.

One of the men started talking so quietly that Desh and Abigail couldn't hear what he said.

"Harry?" Jeb called to the shadows.

Judge Harry Haney came from the shadows and said confidently, "What's going on, boys? Is there something I can help you with?"

Again the quiet voice spoke, and a suited man motioned

for Jeb and Judge Haney to get into one of the cars. In the meantime, a couple of the other men had been talking to the truck drivers. One of the officials gave a signal and the two dump trucks started up and moved toward the opening of the cave, followed by the black Cadillacs.

"Well, that's that," Desh said when the roar of engines had finally quieted. "The next few days should be busy for Judge Harry Haney. I doubt he'll have time to even give his goons any directions. But just in case he does, I want you to keep a very low profile."

"So apparently Harry and Jeb don't even know that an entire room is right above their heads?" Abigail marveled.

"Apparently not. They know that there are other rooms, they just don't know where or how to get to them. They suspect that the openings are on your property. That's why they're so determined to get it. But I don't think they'd ever guess your barn sits right smack on top of what they're looking for." Desh chuckled at the thought.

"So how do these two rooms fit in with the tunnel that runs between our properties?" Abigail asked.

"I'm not sure. But it appears that this cave and the tunnel are above the one where the tires are. There must be an opening of some kind in the tunnel that we haven't discovered yet. A crevice or opening that allows the noise from the trucks to be heard so well. We'll have to look more carefully for it.

"Speaking of which, why don't we go examine the room where we came in," Desh said, leading the way back through the magnificent cave they'd come through.

"This would make a great tourist attraction," he mused.

"I was just thinking the same thing," Abigail said. "This cave system might put Leaky Springs on the map one day." Abigail's imagination worked overtime for a few moments, thinking about all the ramifications of owning a lucrative business like that.

But trepidation replaced excitement as they made their way into the much smaller room and headed toward the table. Abigail knew in her heart she was about to learn something very important about her mom.

Desh shined the light on the metal box. It looked to be about twelve inches wide and approximately twelve inches tall. He motioned for Abigail to open it. Hesitantly, she reached for the lid and slowly lifted it.

A stack of paper greeted them. The first of the papers were more drawings of cave rooms. Farther down in the box was a stack of letters held together by a rubber band. And at the very bottom of the box was a small book.

Abigail's pounding heart thumped in her ears. She realized she held a diary. Her mom's diary. Tears blurred her eyes as she carefully, tenderly opened it, feeling as if she were trespassing on private property. Yet unable to stop herself.

A piece of loose paper fluttered to the tabletop. Abigail picked it up and held it to the light. It read:

If someone is reading this, then I'm probably not alive.

Chapter 19

"Do you want to read the diary in private?" Desh asked, after they'd made their way back to his house and were standing in the kitchen. He felt fairly safe in coming back to the house, now that Judge Haney was temporarily being distracted.

Weariness engulfed Abigail from her previous two-day ordeal. Her body longed to go upstairs and snuggle into the big bed and sleep for hours. But her emotions insisted that she read the words her mom had written so many years ago.

"No. I don't want to be alone when I read this. I want you with me," she said.

Longing to hold and comfort her, Desh settled for taking her arm and leading her to the sofa. They settled on the sofa, bodies touching like contented lovers. Desh gloried in the fact that Abigail seemed so comfortable with being this close to him. Sitting this close in the living room, in the bright light, was a lot different than sitting this close in a damp, dark cave.

He placed the metal box on the floor and took the diary out. He handed it to Abigail and watched emotions play over her face as she held it, almost afraid to open it.

Finally, taking a long, shuddering breath, Abigail started to read.

I have made a horrible mistake. I have made a pact with the devil. I think I've actually sold my soul to him. That wouldn't bother me so much, but I may have sold the soul of my child to him, too. Harry Haney is an evil man.

The very first entry of her mom's diary gave Abigail cold chills. She knew she was holding information that would help her destroy Judge Harry Haney. She'd hoped and prayed for this kind of information, but she never dreamed it would come from her own mother, who had died when she, Abigail, was just a small child.

She was about to read again when the sound of a car stopping in the driveway caught their attention. Desh quickly placed the diary back into the metal box and handed it to Abigail.

"Go upstairs and lock the door to your room," he directed, before even checking to see who had stopped outside.

Abigail hurried to her room and locked the door behind her. She could hear Desh's voice downstairs, but couldn't understand what he was saying.

Taking the diary from the box, she stuck the box into a back corner of the closet. She carefully slid the diary between the wall and the huge chest of drawers that held her clothes. Then she sat on the bed and waited.

She desperately wanted to ease the door open and try to hear the conversation, but knew any sound from her could be detrimental. She felt like a coward sitting up here and letting Desh face the enemy, if, indeed, it was the enemy at the door.

Suddenly she heard Desh's voice become louder. "So that's it? I've wasted my time following that scumball for several years, and he just walks?"

Other voices—quiet, calming voices that Abigail couldn't understand—answered Desh.

"I don't care!" he shouted back at them. "This is bullshit! He dumps tires illegally, and on someone else's property, and gets away with a fine?"

The other voices said a few more things, then left. Abigail had begun to wonder if Desh had gone with them, but finally he called up the stairs for her to come down.

He stood at the window, rubbing the back of his neck, when Abigail entered the room.

"What happened?" she asked.

He turned slowly and looked at her. She saw the pain on his face before he spoke.

"I've failed you, Abigail. I thought I was really doing something to help you bring down that sorry, no-good piece of trash, but he's getting away with it."

"Desh. I couldn't hear from upstairs. Please tell me what happened."

"That was the EPA reps. They've been with Harry Haney all morning. It seems that since this is his first offense, he can pay a fine, get a permit to dispose of solid waste material, and continue in business. He promised them he'd clean up the tires and dispose of them correctly. But we know that's a lie. He'll keep dumping the tires just like he's doing."

Bitterness etched lines in Desh's face, causing him to appear much older than he was. Abigail had to remind herself that he'd just buried his father. He'd had a very stressful few weeks.

"I figured all along that he wouldn't get much punishment for dumping the tires, but I really thought it would be more than what he got! I thought maybe he'd be put in jail for six months or a year, and that would give me time to proceed with my other investigation."

"What other investigation?" Abigail asked, wondering what he was on to.

"I'm not even sure. There's just more going on with the judge than illegal tire dumping. I can't seem to get anyone to talk about it, though."

Before she could answer, he stopped and stood gazing at Abigail. "You know what this means. He'll really be after you, now. We've got to get you out of here!"

The ringing of the phone interrupted his urgent statement. He glanced at it but let it go. "From now on, let the machine get it until we hear who's calling," he instructed.

The caller hung up without leaving a message. "That's them. They're checking to see if we're here. Come on, we've got to go now."

"But Desh, where?" Abigail asked, even as he led her from the house, locking the door behind them.

Once they were in his car and heading down the driveway, he answered her. "I'm taking you to Birmingham. They'll never find you in a big city like that. We'll check you into a hotel until I can figure a way through this."

"No."

"What do you mean, no?"

"No. I won't run. It's time for me to make my stand, Desh. I really appreciate all you've done to help me, but this isn't your fight. This is my fight. I was the one who was framed and sent to prison. It's my property that they want, not yours. Oh, yes. It *is* yours, isn't it?"

"It's *our* property, Abigail."

"Yes, but Harry Haney doesn't know that, so it's me he wants to kill in order to get it."

Desh screeched to a stop so quickly that Abigail threw her hands to the dash of the car to stop the impact, even though she had her seatbelt on.

"You know, I'm acting pretty dense to be a lawyer," Desh

said. "You're absolutely right. So I know how to call the dogs off of you." He took his cell phone from his pocket.

"Desh! What are you doing?" Abigail reached for the phone. Desh caught her hand in his and held it while he punched a number with the thumb of the hand that held the phone.

"Harry?" he said, when the line was answered. "This is Desh Elliot. I've been meaning to thank you for the beautiful wreath you sent to my dad's funeral." He paused while the voice on the other end said something, then continued, "Well, I really appreciate those kind words, and I'm sure my dad would, too. But there's something else I want to discuss with you. I understand that you want to buy Abigail Avery's property? Well, she doesn't own that property any more. I've owned it for a few years now. And it's not for sale. So you need to call your goons off of her. I guess if you're going to kill someone for it, you'll have to kill me." He closed his cell phone without waiting for an answer.

Abigail looked at Desh in stunned silence. He'd put his life on the line for her.

"Don't worry, Abigail. Unlike your parents and grandparents, I have a will. If anything happens to me, everything I own goes to you," he said, pulling the car back onto the road.

The magnitude of what Desh had just done immobilized Abigail for a few minutes. Tears welled up in her eyes and threatened to spill over. If she'd ever doubted his sincerity, and she had at times, she didn't doubt it now.

Finally, gaining her composure, she said, "I want to go to Mabelle's."

"Mabelle's? Why? Abigail, that's right in the middle of town. That's like walking into the lion's den."

"Well, if Mabelle has accomplished what she was supposed to, the lion is close to being declawed."

"What on earth are you talking about?" Desh asked.

"Just take me there and I'll explain."

As Desh headed toward Mabelle's Salon, Abigail said, "I think she'll be at home today. She was supposed to cancel all her appointments for a few days while she did some research."

When they pulled into Mabelle's driveway, they saw Sheriff Lucas's patrol car parked close to the house.

"Now that's odd," Desh said. "Why is he here?"

"I think—I hope he's been helping Mabelle. She said she was going to ask him for help after I told her about our visit with him."

Mabelle opened the door before they reached it. "Come on in," she said. Excitement shined in her eyes. "You won't believe what we've discovered the past two days! I tried to call you earlier, but got your answering machine. I didn't dare leave you a message, for fear the wrong person would hear it."

"So that was you," Desh observed. "We were there, but didn't answer it for the same reason."

"So you've heard what went down about the tires?" William asked.

"Yes. Can you believe that?"

"They'll really come after Abigail, now," William said.

"Not after what Desh just did," Abigail offered.

"What was that?" William asked, looking quizzically at Desh.

"I just tried to lead Harry in a different direction," Desh hedged.

"By telling him that he owned my property," Abigail said.

"Desh! That put your life in danger!" Mabelle exclaimed. "You must really love Abigail a lot to do something like that."

Abigail looked quickly at Mabelle. Was she trying to get a confession from him?

"Well, Mabelle, when a man loves a woman, he'll do a

lot to prove it. You know that now, don't you?" William Lucas fairly beamed at Mabelle.

"Yes, William, I know that now," Mabelle said, and went to stand in the circle of his arm before looking knowingly at Abigail. "William has asked me to marry him. It seems he's loved me for a long time. I thought we were just friends, because I had myself convinced that I loved someone else. I've discovered in the past few days that the man I love is right here waiting for me to open my eyes and see him."

"Congratulations!" Desh and Abigail offered the couple.

Then Abigail asked Mabelle, "Did you manage to contact Becky and Jane?"

"Yes. And from what they told us, we don't even need to ask the others. I'm sure the others will be brought in for the trial."

"Would someone mind telling me what's going on?" Desh asked.

"He doesn't know?" Mabelle and William asked at the same time.

"I haven't had a chance to tell him," Abigail said, not going into all she and Desh had just been through.

"Everybody sit down. This may take a while," Mabelle said.

"We don't have time to sit and chat," Desh said. "I have to get Abigail out of this town and to safety. Harry will have his goons after both of us, now. So she's not even safe with me."

Abigail took a seat on the sofa and motioned for Desh to sit beside her. "We don't have to run anymore, Desh. Soon the *Honorable* Judge Harry Haney will be wanting to run from us."

The look of bewilderment on Desh's face brought a smile to Abigail's lips.

"This is going to be hard for me to talk about, but it's time both of us talked about it," she said, looking at Mabelle.

"Not long before my mom died, she and I visited Judge Harry Haney's chambers. I didn't know why we were there, but for some reason, my mom left me alone with him. He asked me if I wanted some candy and some juice. When he brought me the juice, he spilled it on me. Poured it on me, to be exact. Then he made a big deal of my clothes being wet and that I'd get sick if I didn't take them off.

"I fought him, but he finally got my dress off and told me that I could wear one of his robes. He said I could be judge for a while. I didn't like the way the robe smelled, but he forced me to put it on, anyway.

"Then he started going on about how cute I looked and that he just had to make some pictures of me. Of course the robe swallowed my small body, but he'd pull it off of one shoulder and let it hang down, or fix it in some other seductive way. I didn't know it was seductive at the time—I just thought he was stupid. But he always managed to have it open in the front so my "pretty panties" could show, as he put it."

She paused briefly at Desh's quickly indrawn breath. His face was so red she was afraid he was going to have a stroke, but she had to keep talking. She had never told anyone the entire story, so once she got started she couldn't seem to stop.

"When he finished taking all the pictures he wanted, he told me to put my wet dress back on, that my mom would be there soon. Then he told me if I ever told anyone about this, he'd kill my mom.

"While I was in prison, I learned a lot about child porn, pedophiles, child molesters, and the like. I started to wonder just what our good judge did behind closed doors. The more I thought about it, the more I believed that Judge Harry Haney was into that kind of thing.

"Then when I first got home, Mabelle indicated that she really hated him. Come to find out, he did her the same way. Mabelle, do you want to take it from here?"

"I'll be happy to," Mabelle said. "It feels so good to finally get this out in the open and to bring that son-of-bitch down! He did the exact same thing to me. Then, after he had the photos developed, he showed them to my mom and told her that if she didn't do exactly as he asked her, any time he asked her, he'd have her arrested for selling photos of her own daughter. He told her he'd say he found the photos in her house. My mom told me this on her deathbed. She wept like a baby and apologized for being too weak to do anything about him.

"When William and I talked with Becky and Jane, they admitted that he'd done the same thing with them. Took pictures of their little girls and threatened them with the same thing. That's why they were on the jury. He'd call in the people he had a hold on whenever he needed them. Becky and Jane said he'd probably done the same thing to the other women, but it may have been their grandchildren. Then after your trial he paid them off and told them to get out of town and that he never wanted to see them again."

"That dirty, low-down bastard!" Desh was on his feet now. "You two are going to file charges against him, aren't you? And what about the others? Do you think they'll cooperate?"

"I'm sure they will," William said. "The two we talked with seemed extremely happy that this was about to come out."

"That explains the women, but what does he have on the men who also convicted Abigail?" Desh wondered aloud.

"There's more," Abigail interjected. She had their complete attention.

"The other night when I was held captive in the courthouse and managed to escape? When I first got out of the room I was in, I went upstairs because I saw a light shining under a door. I thought I might be able to escape that way. But I wound up in Judge Haney's closet."

The gasps of disbelief stopped her for a moment. "He was

still in his office," she continued. "Working on his computer. At least, that's what I thought he was doing until I looked at the computer more closely. He was watching what looked like to be nude children posing in different provocative positions. He never knew I was around. I managed to go back down the stairs and out the back door.

"Personally, I think he's probably involved in a child porn ring and the other guys who do his beck and call are probably involved with him. He probably holds that over their heads."

"FBI," Desh said, satisfaction resounding in his voice. "We've got the dirty bastard. We'll call the FBI and they can swarm his office, confiscate his computer and those of all his cohorts. They have the authority to do that. This is our ace in the hole. Abigail, I hope you know what you saw. I'd hate for us to be wrong about this and for him to be able to go free on a false arrest."

"Oh, I know what I saw. I thought I was going to throw up and give myself away, it made me so sick, and brought back such horrible memories."

"William, will you call the FBI and get them here tomorrow? I want to get Abigail out of here for the time being."

"No!"

"Abigail, be reasonable! They could kill you before the night is over," Desh said.

"No. They won't kill me. And I want to be there when the FBI takes him down. I want him to look into my face and know that I played a major role in his demise.

"I have to do this, Desh. I've waited ten long years to watch this happen."

Chapter 20

Abigail, Desh, Mabelle and William sat in William's patrol car and watched several unmarked vehicles pull into the small town of Leaky Springs. When it was time for them to make their move, the FBI agents were to radio Sheriff Lucas and let him know, so the small party could be on the scene when they brought the judge out.

Desh clutched one of Abigail's hands as if he'd never let it go. She could tell he was wound so tightly that he could hardly stay in the car.

Desh and Abigail had left Mabelle's last night and gone back to his house, taken the diary from behind the chest of drawers, and spent the night in the cave, in the little room where her mom had apparently run for safety on the many occasions she feared for her life.

Abigail and Desh had spent the night sitting on the floor of the cave, reading the entire diary. It wasn't terribly long, but it had most of the answers to Abigail's questions. Most of them. She was sure the rest of the answers would come out in the trial of Judge Harry Haney.

According to her mom's diary, Harry Haney had, indeed, threatened her with the same story of finding photos of her child, just like he had the other women. He seemed to pick on weak women who didn't have the courage or strength to fight for themselves.

Somehow he'd found out that her mom had a talent for drawing maps and that she also knew the cave system like the back of her hands from spending a lot of time in the caves with her dad, who was a spelunker. So he'd forced her to draw the elaborate maps of the cave system for him.

But the biggest surprise was the entry that explained the money. It seemed that the judge insisted on paying her mom for drawing the maps, so that if she ever accused him of forcing her to do it, he could come back with the argument that she was being paid, so obviously she wasn't being forced. Each time he'd give her money, he'd write himself a receipt and make her sign it.

Abigail had to laugh when she found out why the maps and money were in her dad's old chair. *He's already drunk by the time he hits that chair, every night,* the entry read, *and he refuses to let me destroy the chair, so I figured that would be the safest place for the money.*

The last entry had been to Abigail. It brought tears to her eyes to remember it.

My darling child. I fear I'll never see you grow up. Your dad is so jealous of me, and his angry fits are getting worse. He thinks I'm having an affair because I stay gone so much during the day working on the drawings. I can't tell him the truth for fear that Judge Haney will have me sent to prison, as he promised. And I can't spend the money to leave because I know Judge Haney will hunt me down.

Your dad became a drunk soon after we married, so he knows that my love for him is almost gone. I know he blames himself, but he's trying to put the blame on me. Be happy, my child, wherever you are when you read this.

Abigail wiped at the tear that ran down her face, and Desh caught her action. He squeezed her hand and whispered, "It's almost over. Soon you can start to rebuild your life."

"Soon I can start to *build* a life," she corrected him. "I've never had one to rebuild."

"We're going in," a voice came over the radio. And suddenly the courthouse steps were swarming with men and women heading inside the stately old building.

The four in the car hurriedly got out and took their place at the bottom of the steps. After what seemed like an eternity, the entourage reappeared. A couple of the men had Judge Harry Haney by the arm. Several others were carrying computers. Apparently they had confiscated all the computers in the building.

As they approached Abigail's group, the agents leading the judge stopped, at Desh's motion. Desh had advised Abigail not to make any threats or accusations that weren't true, but that she could say anything to the judge that was factual.

Abigail looked into the defiant eyes of the man who had wrecked so many lives in this small town, and no telling how many of the neighboring towns. She watched, with satisfaction, as recognition dawned on the face of the judge.

She'd dreamed about this moment for ten long years. Had fantasized about what she would say. She'd even considered spitting in his face. But nothing she'd ever thought about could have prepared her for the feeling of power that now swept over her.

Suddenly she knew that she was in control of her life for the first time. She felt no fear of the man who stood before her. She'd finally be able to lie down at night and not have to think about him. She was free. Not just from the physical prison where she'd spent ten years, but from the mental prison that she'd been in most of her life. Free.

"*Your Honor,*" her voice dripped with contempt, "I hope you rot in hell."

"Just like your old man," Judge Haney smirked as the FBI agents led him away. "Too proud to kiss the right ass."

Several months had passed since Judge Haney's arrest. An
extensive child porn ring had been uncovered that took in several counties. Ned and Jeb Thompson had been part of the ring. But the other men who had served on the jury that convicted Abigail had been as framed as she'd been.

Harry Haney turned out to be even more devious than anyone could know. He'd actually had one of his people go into the homes of Sam Tanner, Jim Duncan—and later Josh Duncan—and Dan Tucker and install porn on their computers, then blackmail them because it was there, just as he'd done the women with the photos of their daughters.

In her wildest dreams, Abigail could never have conjured up the scene that unfolded before her.

Judge Haney on trial. His face still held a look of cocky confidence and denial, in spite of all the facts that were being brought out about him. He still thought he was above the law.

Desh was awesome as the prosecuting attorney. He had shown just how determined and brilliant he was by making arrangements for a female judge to try the case. Finally he was able to fulfill the purpose that he'd arranged his life for. To put Judge Harry Haney away for a very long time.

Mabelle, Becky and Jane had testified, and now Desh was saying, "I now call my star witness to the stand."

The courtroom hushed as Abigail walked up to take her oath. Justice was about to be done, and everyone in the room was anxious to see how Abigail Avery would handle the situation.

Abigail looked out into the faces of some of the same townspeople who had sat in this very courtroom and watched her be sentenced to prison. She found and looked into the eyes of each of the jurors who could be there, who had, under the blackmailed influence of Judge Haney, sentenced her to ten years of prison. Each of them had come to her and apologized and begged her forgiveness. And they all had thanked her for what she was doing to put a stop to the evil man who had controlled and ruined their lives for so many years.

And then she looked directly into the eyes of the evil Judge Harry Haney. A sense of power filtered through her as she saw reality in his eyes. He faltered and almost looked away from her direct gaze, but then determinedly stared back at her.

Abigail Avery's eyes didn't waver. She captured and held his gaze while she repeated, slowly and deliberately, the story she'd told Desh at Mabelle's house. Then she told about the night her father had been murdered. How the gun had been taken from the barn and used to kill her father, and was lying on top and across his hands when she'd found him. And yet, she'd been sent to prison for a crime she couldn't have committed.

When all was said and done, Judge Harry Haney would spend the rest of his life behind bars.

"There you are," Desh said, coming up behind her. "Are you ready to go home?"

Abigail took one last look around her old room. She'd wanted to come here today as part of her healing therapy. It felt odd to be able to move around her home without fear that someone would shoot at her through the window, or surprise her by walking in the door and catching her. Or dread that her dad would come in and get angry because of something he found undone.

As she'd moved from room to room, she was surprised at

a few good memories that forced their way past the bad ones. She felt that the more she came to grips with her childhood, and the more she got to know who the real Abigail Avery was, more of the good memories would surface.

She found that she didn't even hate her father as much as she thought she did. After reading her mom's diary, she realized her dad was actually a lost soul, himself. The pack of letters in the tin box had been love letters her mom had gotten from him when he was in the Army, before they got married. The sweet words her dad had written to her mom showed a side of him that Abigail had never seen. She understood how her mother could have loved him.

It was a shame he and her grandparents hadn't gotten off on a better footing than they had. Apparently there was something about him worth loving, if her mom had loved him enough to give up her own parents for him.

Abigail knew she'd never know the truth about most of that part of their lives, and that was okay. Some things just weren't meant to be known.

"Yes, I'm ready to go," she said, turning to Desh.

As they walked past the barn, Abigail glanced at the fresh mound of earth in the pasture beside the barn. Desh had helped her bury Betsy's bones. Poor Betsy. Abigail had cried the entire time they'd scooped up Betsy's bones and put them in a wooden box. She shuddered every time she thought of the old cow slowly starving to death, pinned up and alone in that crib.

As if reading her thoughts, Desh reached for Abigail's hand and led her onward to the cave entrance and to his house. She'd walked through the cave to her house this morning. He'd let her go, knowing she needed to be alone with her thoughts.

Once inside the kitchen, Abigail realize he'd made dinner and the table was set. It was an identical replica of the meal and setting he'd made for her the night she got home from prison.

"What's this all about?" Abigail asked.

"I've come to a conclusion, Abigail. I realize that most of your life has been traumatic. I realize that you need time to heal and come to grips with who you are and what you want out of life. I've been trying to force you to love me, but you don't even know how to love, yet. I thought that my love for you could heal all of your wounds and that my love for you would be enough for both of us. I know now that it doesn't matter how much I love you, you have to figure out what you want from life.

"So I want to relive your first night home. I want to welcome you home, then give you space to enjoy your freedom. I'm moving out of the house for a while. Maybe for good, if you can't find it in your heart to love me. I bought this house for us. For you, mostly. It means nothing to me without you in it. I don't want it without you in it. I may not live in it, but when I think about you, I want to think about you in this house.

"So, live here for a while, my Abigail. Find yourself. But I'm not going too far away. I'll keep pestering you. I'll keep coming around and begging you to love me. I'm kind of pathetic that way."

"Are you finished with that fine speech, Dashing Desh Elliot?" Abigail asked.

"I think so," he said, sheepishly.

"Then let me have my say. I'm sure my mom loved me. But I was so young when she died that I don't remember what love felt like. And nobody else had ever made any attempt to show me what it felt like until I came home from prison and you came into my life.

"For the first time someone was saying wonderful words to me that didn't have any meaning. Sure, I knew the words. I watched movies in prison. I read a few books with those words in them. But I'd never had them said to me.

"But you backed up your words with actions. While I was

away, you arranged your entire life in order to help me. When I came home, you gave up your safety to help me. When it came down to it, you were even willing to die for me.

"You didn't just tell me those wonderful words, Desh. You *showed* me what love is.

"It's not going to be easy, because I'm still learning. I'm sure there'll be days when I won't believe that you love me. But I want to believe you. I want you to teach me.

"I think I love you. If wanting to spend the rest of my life with you is love, then I do. If wanting to have your arms around me forever is love, then I do. If wanting to give my body to you is—"

But his lips on hers stopped whatever she'd meant to say.

Epilogue

"What do you think?" Desh asked, taking his hard hat off and walking toward Abigail. He'd just come from the old barn, which was being restored and enlarged.

"That looks really wonderful, Desh," Abigail said, welcoming his kiss and the arm he slipped around her shoulders.

The barn would be the opening to the cave entrance, for tourists to pass through on their way to explore the caves. Abigail's house had already been remodeled and turned into offices to accommodate the business end of the Leaky Springs Caves tourist attraction. Lighting was in the process of being installed in parts of the caves to illuminate some of the more beautiful, unusual spots.

Hopefully within the year they would be open for guests to visit and tour the caves. Their goal was to keep the small town atmosphere of Leaky Springs, yet draw tourists in to boost the economy of the area. Since this was the first cave system tourist attraction in Mississippi, they were a little concerned that tourists might come in droves and threaten the small-town atmosphere they wanted to maintain. But it was a chance they were willing to take.

The dumped tires had been cleaned up and hauled away, at the expense of Judge Harry Haney's estate. By the time that project was finished, his ill-gained fortune had disappeared. It was rumored that *The* Mrs. Harry Haney had divorced him and was looking for another rich sucker to marry.

Desh ran his hand through Abigail's mass of golden-red hair, which had grown back in the past year, and asked the question he'd been putting off. "What did the doctor say?" Abigail had been really tired, lately, and had gone to the doctor today to find out if anything was wrong. Desh had wanted to go with her, but she'd insisted that he wasn't needed.

"He said we need to start picking out names," she said, and squealed as Desh lifted her off her feet with a loud whoop, then rained kisses all over her face.

About the Author

Pat Ballard lives in Nashville, TN. She writes motivational romance novels to show that plus-size women can be just as sexy, romantic and exciting as their slim sisters.

Visit Pat on the web at www.patballard.com. Sign up for her free e-mail newsletter, *The Queen's Proclamation*, at www.pearlsong.com/pat_ballard.htm.

Look for her other books published by Pearlsong Press— *Dangerous Curves Ahead: Short Stories, Wanted: One Groom, Nobody's Perfect, His Brother's Child,* and *A Worthy Heir*—at your favorite online and offline bookstores, as well as at www.pearlsong.com.

For news and updates about other Pearlsong Press books and authors, subscribe to the free e-mail newsletter, *The Pearlsong Letter*, at www.pearlsong.com/subscribe.htm, or visit The Pearlsong Letter blog at www.pearlsongpress.com.